"Well, good night," she said

Shari's lips were slightly pinched and he felt the weight of awkwardness pressing on him. Oh, hell. Being an idiot hadn't killed him yet. "So, am I ever going to see you naked again?"

Anger and a touch of hurt sparked in her eyes. "Not in this—"

Luke cut her off before she could finish, knowing he didn't want her making claims that he had no intention of letting her keep. He grabbed her shoulders and pulled her to him, kissing her hard to cut off her words, then softening his lips until her squeak of protest turned into a sigh.

He pulled away slowly, enjoying the slightly stunned expression on Shari's flushed face. She was so ripe and womanly and so exactly what he needed at this moment.

She whispered slowly, as though the word was a playing card she'd forgotten she was holding. "Lifetime."

"Don't count on it," he promised.

Dear Reader,

Sometimes, when I can't sleep at night, I start dreaming up story ideas. *By the Book* is one of those stories from one of those nights. I crept downstairs to my computer and wrote the first couple of scenes when the house was quiet and my imagination could roam free. I knew by morning that I had a new Blaze novel on my hands. It had all the elements I love in a book. A fun and outrageous meet, characters I wanted to get to know better—and I could tell these two were going to be hot.

Also, Luke is a writer. It was a payback to give him some late-night-insomnia writing time—with interesting consequences.

I hope you enjoy the results of one night's insomnia as much as I enjoyed writing about it. I have to say, one of the nice things about finishing a book is catching up on my sleep—until the next idea comes along.

As always, I love to hear from readers. You can reach me on the Web at www.nancywarren.net or drop me a line at P.O. Box 37035, North Vancouver, B.C. V7N 4M0, Canada.

Happy reading,

Nancy

Books by Nancy Warren

BY THE BOOK

Nancy Warren

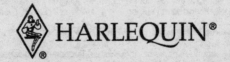

HARLEQUIN®

TORONTO • NEW YORK • LONDON
AMSTERDAM • PARIS • SYDNEY • HAMBURG
STOCKHOLM • ATHENS • TOKYO • MILAN • MADRID
PRAGUE • WARSAW • BUDAPEST • AUCKLAND

This book is dedicated to Wendy Warren, my first fan from
Down Under, and also to Viggo Muhlig. Thanks for the walls.

And thanks to the wonderful women of Nancy's Warren
at eHarlequin.com who come to visit every day.
Thanks for all the laughs and encouragement.

I love you all!

ISBN 0-373-79089-9

BY THE BOOK

Copyright © 2003 by Nancy Warren.

1

SHARI WILSON wanted to kiss the dyslexic postal worker who serviced her vintage brick apartment building in Seattle's Capitol Hill. He'd mixed up her mail again.

Sandwiched between her own letters for S. Wilson, Suite 325, was a bulky brown paper package addressed to L. Lawson, Suite 235. She'd have another excuse to see Luke Lawson, megahunk. She hugged the package to her, as giddy as a schoolgirl with a crush.

Okay, she was a *schoolteacher* with a crush. And what a crush. Her downstairs neighbor made her shiver. It was a combination of a charming smile, tall, rangy body and a twinkle in his sleepy green eyes that just hinted at devilry between the sheets.

They'd been exchanging mixed mail for months now. In all the misdirected letters, she'd noted nothing was addressed to anyone else in his apartment, and there was no sign of a female when she'd delivered mail to his door, so it seemed logical to deduce he was single.

And hot.

Just as she was single.

And hot.

Getting hotter every time she thought of L. Lawson just a floor below her and one suite over in 235.

Fate, in the form of the portly postie, had thrown them repeatedly together and the zing of attraction had been immediate and, she thought, mutual. The last couple of times Luke had come to the door tousled and stubble-cheeked, his heavy-lidded eyes gazing at her as intimately as though she and Luke had just made love. Oh, what those eyes could do to a woman's blood pressure.

So why, apart from seduction by eye contact during their neighborly exchange-mail-and-chitchat sessions, hadn't L. Lawson made any kind of move to get to know her better?

She bit her lip as she bypassed the elevator and jogged up the stairs to her floor. Maybe he was shy, or uncertain of her feelings or status.

Perhaps it was time she took charge of the situation and let him know both her feelings—attracted, very attracted, and her status—single. Very single.

The easiest way to give him the message was to ask him out. Nothing too intimate, just a movie or Chinese or pizza. A simple get-together that would give them a chance to become better acquainted.

She would run down with his mail, casual as can be, and say, "Hey, I was just going to grab something to eat. If you're not doing anything, why don't you join me?"

Yes. That was the way—easy, no pressure. If he turned her down she'd know where she stood and could ditch the adolescent fantasies that had begun to creep into her mind. Letting herself into her apartment, she snorted. There was nothing adolescent about her fantasies. They were definitely of the *not approved for audiences under the age of eighteen* variety.

She dumped her bag of marking on the dining table and picked up Luke's package. Taking a deep breath, she decided to go for it. She'd reply to the erotic messages his eyes had been sending her way. She'd ask him out.

Tonight.

A once-over in the bathroom mirror reminded her that teaching English to a bunch of high school students was no day at the spa. She couldn't go anywhere without a quick shower. While she was lathered up under a warm spray of water she decided she might as well shave her legs.

After drying off, she brushed her teeth, fixed her hair, applied fresh makeup and headed into the bedroom. She reached for jeans, then changed her mind. She was sick of jeans.

A nice flirty skirt just jumped right out of her wardrobe and into her arms. She added a torso-hugging top in her favorite purple, some fun, dangly earrings and she was ready. She reached into the bottom of her closet for strappy sandals and caught herself. She didn't want to look as if she'd dressed up for Luke, when nothing could be further from the truth.

Shari grabbed her Birkenstocks instead. Yes, they made just the right statement. She retrieved the package, then noticed a blob of something on her skirt.

Back to the bathroom. She put the brown envelope down, turned on the tap then reached for her hand-washing soap. Ach, she needed a new bar and it was under the sink somewhere. On her hands and knees she rummaged through the bathroom cleaners, boxes of first-aid items, that time-of-the-month stuff, her travel bag for toiletries. Ah, there was the soap, right at the back. She found a clean facecloth, too, and rose.

And gasped.

Damn. The faucet was leaking again. Water trickled from its base gathering on the countertop in a pool that had reached Luke's package and soaked into the kraft paper. She grabbed up the brown envelope and gingerly poked at the wet end. It was a little soggy, but surely there hadn't been time for the water to soak whatever was inside. Felt like a book. Uh-oh.

Best to get it into Luke's hands before the moisture penetrated. She decided to leave cleaning her skirt until later and just scraped off the blob with a fingernail.

She grabbed her keys, her black leather satchel and the package, let herself out of her apartment and ran down one flight of stairs to Luke's floor.

In no time she was standing outside his door breathing faster than anyone should who'd only run *down* a single flight of stairs. She took a deep gulp of air, rehearsed her casual dinner invitation and knocked.

Silence.

It hadn't occurred to her that he wouldn't be home. He was always home. She knew from their casual conversation that he was a journalist—she'd even seen his byline in the local paper. Almost as soon as she'd had the thought, she heard the lock scrape and then the door opened.

And Luke Lawson cast his usual erotic spell over her. He was, without doubt, the sexiest man she'd ever seen. No matter how many times she saw him, his in-your-face sex appeal always struck her. And, just as reliably, her heart jumped and started working overtime, pumping blood to every erogenous zone in her body—and a few zones that were borderline but just wanted to join the party.

The wonderful sizzle of attraction danced and popped through her blood and along her nerve endings as she gazed at him. It wasn't just the devilish glint in his green eyes, hinting at intimacies they'd never shared, but so easily could. And it wasn't just the dimple in his chin, or the disheveled dark brown hair that reminded her of lazy Saturday mornings in bed, or the broad shoulders and muscular chest. It was, she decided, the way all the elements of his appearance went together.

Just right.

His mouth broke into a welcoming smile when he saw her and the package she held out. "Don't tell me he did it again?"

He didn't sound annoyed at the mail mix-up. He sounded as delighted as she felt.

She tried to keep the grin off her own face as she handed him his package. "Yep. He did it again."

She wanted to say something to him, of that she was absolutely certain, but what was it? She gazed at him, feeling the powerful force of his animal magnetism drawing her closer.

His gaze skimmed her body, which immediately upped the sizzle wattage. "You look great," he said. "Going someplace special?"

Oh, that was it. Her brain clicked back into place. She was going to ask him out. She glanced down at herself with what she hoped was a this-old-thing? expression. "No, nothing special. In fact I was wondering—"

She got no further. A damp squishy sound interrupted, followed by a loud thunk. She glanced down to see the wet end of the package split and a large paperback book fall, in what seemed like slow motion, to the floor.

The book—a garish-looking, large-size paperback—landed face-up. The title, in black against a glossy red background, was in type so huge she could have read it from a block away.

Sex For Total Morons: A How-To Guide.

She couldn't stop staring at the thing pulsing its neon message from the floor. A blush rose on her cheeks. It couldn't be. If Luke sent away for a book like this...well, that would mean... No. It couldn't be.

She stared at the title, as though if she concentrated hard enough the words might rearrange themselves into *Home Woodworking for the Handyman* or *Financial Planning for Beginners*. But even when she blinked, the words didn't change; *Sex For Total Morons: A How-To Guide* imprinted itself like an X ray on the back of her eyelids.

What a disappointment. She didn't know if she was more embarrassed for Luke, that he needed a how-to manual, or for herself, that she'd discovered his humiliating secret. All she knew was her face was at least as red as the book jacket.

After one of those awful moments that seem to stretch for centuries, she risked an upward glance to find Luke fiddling with the remains of the brown envelope, a duller shade of red coloring his own cheeks.

"I'm sorry," she blurted. "It was my fault. The...the envelope got wet. I meant to warn you. I was just, um, washing something in the sink and...well my faucet leaks..." Oh, Lord. She was sounding like a total moron herself. She pressed her lips together to stop her own babbling.

"I don't suppose..." He cleared his throat. "I don't suppose you'd believe me if I told you that book's for a friend."

"It was addressed to you," she reminded him, feeling worse by the second.

He sighed. "There is that."

Every second the awkwardness between them increased. Disappointment was a lead weight in her stomach. It wasn't that she'd even planned on going to bed with him, she barely knew the man. But, well, the possibility had always crackled in the air between them.

At least she'd thought so. Now she had a feeling she'd let her own fantasies turn him into God's gift to women. Something he clearly wasn't. Not that she minded, of course. He was still a very nice man.

It was just that knowing he needed a how-to book took all the fun out of things. It was like easing open a gorgeously wrapped box of chocolates and finding nothing but Turkish delight—blech. Going to see Kenneth Branagh play Hamlet and discovering he was sick and the no-talent third understudy was taking his place. Picking up a book and... *Oh, God. Don't even go there.*

Her discovery wasn't earth-shattering. Just really, really disappointing.

As each uncomfortable second passed, the urge to escape grew stronger.

"Anyway." She forced a bright smile. "I should get going. I've got this, uh..." She flapped her hands around, looking for a graceful exit line, some dreadfully important engagement she had to rush off to, some... "thing."

The glance he sent her reminded her that she'd just told him she didn't have anything special on tonight. In fact, she'd said, she was wondering...and had been about to ask him out. Oh, damn. Her addled brain couldn't think of any graceful way out of the awkwardness. "Well, I'd better be going."

"Sure. Thanks for the—" he cleared his throat again "—package."

"Anytime," she called over her shoulder, already bolting.

LUKE WATCHED HIS SEXY, and seriously flustered, upstairs neighbor run the hundred yard dash to the stairwell, and wondered just how the evening might have ended if the envelope hadn't broken open at that most inopportune moment.

Shaking his head at the vagaries of fate and the U.S. Postal Service, he shut the door and eased to a squat in front of the book. The cover was a bit more in-your-face than he would have liked, but it was certainly eye-catching.

He traced the title, *Sex for Total Morons: A How-To Guide* by Lance Flagstaff. He picked up the heavy tome and whacked himself softly on the forehead. "Lance, buddy. Your timing sucks."

He gazed at the damp, jagged edge of the envelope. If it had only held together a few more minutes... It reminded him of one of the sections in chapter eight, and he shook his head. "Talk about premature ejaculation."

Well, his babe-radar suggested he'd been intriguingly close to having a date tonight, till Lance popped out, uninvited.

Damn. With his latest men's magazine article in the mail, and no looming deadlines for a change, he'd have loved a night on the town. And he couldn't think of anyone he'd rather spend it with than the lady upstairs. Shari Wilson, Suite 325—the reward he'd promised himself when his most crushing deadlines eased.

Luke groaned in frustration, knowing a night with Shari wasn't going to happen anytime soon. Lance had seen to that.

There were places he could go tonight, but all of a sudden he didn't feel like going anywhere. Instead, he went to the fridge in his galley kitchen, popped the top off a beer and returned to the living room where he settled onto the couch to flip through his new book.

"Chapter One. First Impressions." Luke snorted over his beer thinking about Shari's face as she read the title of the book. He'd made an impression on her she'd remember forever. Unfortunately, it wasn't quite the impression he'd hoped for.

He most certainly didn't want to be seen as a guy who needed a how-to book in order to bed a babe.

Why hadn't he just told her the truth?

I wrote the damn book. The words had formed in his mind, but never made it out of his mouth.

He ought to be proud of his first book. Okay, it wasn't the novel he'd always planned to write, but it was an honest-to-God book, with real pages and a cover. He'd certainly felt the urge to confess that he was, in fact, Lance Flagstaff. He could have joked with her about all the fun he'd had inventing that pseudonym and hopefully have watched the disappointment fade from her eyes.

The beer cooled his throat but not his frustration. He was shy about letting anyone in on his little secret. Even though he'd written the instructional book, he wasn't at all convinced a book could teach lovemaking.

Like most men, he imagined, he'd learned to make love to women by trial and error, by finding out from his partners what they liked, by being open about his own preferences.

It had always seemed to work fine. The women he slept with usually came back for more. Quite eagerly, in fact.

Sex education wasn't, in his view, a matter of reading. It was a matter of getting out and doing. Luke felt he'd learned something from every woman he'd been with. And he'd discovered that the sex was always unique, because the combination of bodies, likes and experience was always new. How could you explain all that in a few hundred pages?

How could he explain that there was nothing more sensuous or sexually exciting than asking a woman to show him how she liked to be touched, or stroked, or caressed, then giving her the utmost pleasure. And when a woman was equally open about asking him to share his preferences, he was only too happy to show her what turned his crank. That's how sex worked in his experience, and no book could replace the honest give-and-take of new lovers.

He tapped the longneck against his teeth. Was he a hypocrite? He'd been writing a column and features in men's and women's magazines for years on the subject of sex, usually offering a man's perspective on the dating scene, what turned men on—gee, that one had needed a whole lot of research. All a woman had to say was, "Wanna get naked?" and that did it for most men he knew. He'd attended various seminars and programs, some hokey and some mindbendingly scientific, read countless books in the name of research, interviewed enough sexually active men and women to fill a small country. Through it all, Lance had developed a reputation as an expert on matters sexual.

Then came the book offer. Frankly, he'd been flattered to be approached. Plus, the venture had sounded like fun. It was a nice big project with a nice fat advance, so he'd written *Sex for Total Morons*, secretly wondering if he wasn't helping deforest the planet for nothing.

Can a book teach you how to be a great lover?

The question had plagued him all through the research and writing, and bothered him still. Too bad there was no way to find out if the program he'd outlined in the book actually worked.

About to toss the book to the table beside the couch, he once again saw Shari's pretty face flush as she'd read the title and its implication had sunk into her mind.

Wait a minute!

He sat bolt upright, his eyes bugging out of his head.

Wait just a damned minute there, *Lance*. Maybe there was a way to test the book.

In his colossal arrogance, he'd never explored the possibility that a woman might actually believe *he* needed a book about sexual technique, never mind be willing to help him learn how to have great sex.

But tonight his bruised ego had learned that it was eminently possible. Shari Wilson had hightailed it out of Dodge precisely because she did believe that he, Luke Lawson, had sent away for a brown-paper-wrapped book to teach him how to be a good lover.

When he got past the insult to his male ego, an intriguing possibility teased him.

Mutual attraction hummed in the air every time he and his upstairs neighbor got close to each other, whether exchanging mail or chatting as they passed in the entrance foyer. He'd been thinking about her more than he should, given his recent deadline hell. But every time he saw her, he got caught up in her full-lipped smile, the brown hair that hung in sexy curls past her shoulders, the killer bod and the spirit of fun he'd sensed in her.

In fact, he'd written the last couple of chapters of *Sex for TMs* picturing Shari in every glorious position his eager imagination could invent. He'd felt so intimate as he'd described the hard-edged pleasure a man feels as he drives himself into a woman who's primed and ready for him, that it seemed inevitable he and Shari would soon be lovers.

Tonight she'd appeared at his door like a fantasy brought to life. The sexual heat they were generating with no more than eye contact had made him feel as if he might burst into flame if he so much as touched her. After months of monklike devotion to work, he'd wanted to start wooing his neighbor into bed. And the way she'd returned the heat of his gaze, he'd half convinced himself the wooing wouldn't take long.

Tonight, his body had begged.

Yes, he'd eagerly answered.

Then the book had tumbled to the floor.

Oh, yeah. Based on Shari's reaction, she believed he needed the how-to primer. Which raised some interesting possibilities. Would the lady be open to helping him discover his inner Casanova?

He'd always loved any kind of a challenge, but a challenge wearing a skirt—a short, sassy skirt that bared shapely legs—was his favorite kind.

What would it take to convince Shari to help him test drive his new book?

He rose and began to pace.

Things had started feeling a little stale in his love life the past year or so. Nothing too specific, just that sometimes going home alone at the end of the evening was more fun than taking a woman with him. The company was better.

It wasn't as if he was going to be popping Viagra anytime soon, but the old Johnson wasn't clamoring for action the way it used to. Sometimes, even at the hottest clubs, with the hottest women, he'd feel restless.

Bored even.

The women he went after nearly always said yes. Where was the challenge in that? And Luke was beginning to realize that he'd come to enjoy the chase almost as much as the catch. More, in fact.

He turned and the lamplight bounced off the red cover of his book like a lascivious wink.

Getting a woman into bed when she believed he was a complete loser in the sack would be a challenge unlike any he'd ever faced. Not just any woman, but Shari Wilson with her intelligent, sparkly eyes, trim figure and her recently conceived notion about his sexual prowess—that he didn't have any.

He started to chuckle. If he could convince Shari to work through the how-to manual with him, step-by-step and chapter-by-chapter, he'd be able to tell firsthand whether the book actually worked.

If she stuck with him through the whole book, while he did nothing but what the manual recommended, and, at the end of it, she still wanted to sleep with him, then he could safely consider himself the Hemingway of the how-to book. And the Dr. Ruth of literature.

Getting Shari to agree to his cockamamy plan was not going to be easy.

In fact, it was just this side of impossible—one of the craziest ideas he'd ever hatched. Which was why he liked it so much.

He glanced down and addressed his privates, which really hadn't seen much action lately. "What do you say, are we up for the challenge?"

It seemed to him his answer was self-evident; his body snapped to attention at the thought of seducing Shari.

Now all he needed was a plan of attack.

2

"I HAVE NEVER BEEN so mortified," Shari told her friend Therese Martin over a Mekong bowl at their favorite noodle house. The wok-shaped light fixture cast its broad glow over Therese, who was laughing so hard she was choking on green tea.

Even though they taught at the same high school, they kept all personal conversation for nights out together. The teachers' lounge had no privacy and was a hotbed of gossip—which Shari and Therese, who also happened to be young and single, avoided at all costs.

Therese managed to stop laughing long enough to gasp, "*Sex for Total Morons*. You really picked yourself another winner."

"I know." She couldn't grudge her friend the laugh. If it had happened to anyone else Shari would have thought it was pretty funny, too. "And he seemed so normal. I mean, he's gorgeous, and he's got this totally sexy look about him. I don't get it. Why would a guy like that need a book on how to make love?"

Therese helped herself to more from the serving plate. "That's easy. The better-looking the guy, the less they've ever had to bother learning about women."

The image of Luke, who all but oozed sex appeal, popped into her mind. "What are you talking about?"

"Haven't you ever gone home with a really great-looking guy and all he talks about is himself?"

Shari nodded. Oh, yeah.

"Then they get in bed and it's still all about them. One time I said to this guy, 'I have a clitoris, you know,' and he asked if it was contagious."

Shari choked on a sip of beer. "You made that up."

Her friend raised her eyebrows and gave her a believe-me-baby-I-have-been-there look. "Uh-uh. I'm telling you, those good-looking ones are the worst." Therese munched reflectively. "But get a guy who stood in the wrong line when they were handing out the Viking genes—maybe he's not so tall, a little skinny. He has to work harder to make it with women. Nobody's going to fall in bed with him based on his looks, right?"

"I hate to think women are that shallow, but in theory, I guess you're right."

"So what does he do? If he wants to have sex with women he has to make up for his shortcomings by being more interesting to them in other ways. Maybe he clues in to asking them about themselves instead of always talking about himself. Maybe he figures out how to have a conversation that doesn't involve sports, his job, his great car, whatever his latest ego trip is.

"Now this guy, when he gets a girl in bed, is going to want to make her happy. He's going to ask her what she likes. He's going to learn how to please her.

And he's going to get quite the rep. Because—" she winked "—women talk."

Shari glanced around the restaurant, paying particular attention to the couples. Some were talking animatedly, touching, holding eye contact, sharing food, while other couples looked as though they could barely stay awake. She couldn't immediately see that it was the homely ones having the great conversations. Anyway, something else about Therese's theory was suspect. "Come on. I've seen you with lots of good-looking guys."

"Yeah. I'm as big a sucker for a hunk as the next girl." She sighed. "Then we get in bed and I spend the next hour going over my lesson plan."

Shari laughed, still certain her friend was joking. She thought back on some of Therese's conquests. "What about that skier, Todd? He looked pretty hot."

"Todd was great. In the looks department. In bed with him, I worked out a whole new way to quiz kids on *passé composé*."

"Ouch. Aren't you being a little harsh?"

Therese shrugged. "Maybe there are men who are fabulous-looking and fabulous lovers. I'm not saying it can't happen, I'm just suggesting that some men have a real advantage when the lights go out. Think about it. Which would you rather have? A guy who makes you drool just looking at him? Or one who knows how to do things to your body that turn you into a musical instrument? An orgasmic virtuoso."

Shari munched rice noodles as she considered the possibilities. "It would be nice to have both."

"Yeah. I know. He's the guy we're all looking for,

hon. But he doesn't exist. He's a dream. Your Total Moron guy's a perfect example."

"At least sending away for that book shows he's trying. I mean, somebody must have told him he wasn't making the grade in the bedroom and he's doing something about it. That's good, right?"

"It's great. I'd be interested to see how far he gets. He'll probably read all the guy stuff and skip the female pages."

"Who turned you into such a cynic?"

It was a rhetorical question, so she was surprised when Therese sighed the sigh of the heartbroken and answered, after a long moment, "A guy named Brad."

"I've never heard of him." Which was odd. She thought they'd shared everything.

"Well, my butt's going to sleep. Let's pay up and I'll tell you on the way to the movie. I've got to walk off all this food."

Once outside in the warm spring air, Therese was uncommonly silent. Shari waited, knowing she'd get the story when her friend was ready to tell it.

"At my last school, across town, I started dating the phys ed teacher. He wasn't good-looking at all, and he was the same height as me in bare feet, shorter when I wore heels. But there was something about him."

They crossed at a green light and scooted 'round a couple of squeegee kids necking on the sidewalk.

"I can't explain it. He listened to me, as if what I had to say was fascinating. As if I was fascinating. He paid attention, not looking behind me to see who was coming into the room who might be more exciting. Not droning on about himself all the time. He was funny, too, which I always like in a man.''

''So you found your bliss with a short, funny guy who listened to you.''

''Did I mention he was balding?''

''No, you didn't.''

''He was. But we became friends and one thing led to another. Next thing I'm in bed with this guy. I swear I turned the light on after an hour just to make sure it was the same man in my bed. I mean, he was…incredible.''

''Okay, I need to start looking for short, funny, balding men. Shouldn't be too tough.''

''It's not a joke, Shari. Brad had moves on him that…'' She tossed her head back, and her long wavy black hair swayed behind her. ''Phew! I'm telling you that man should be in the tongue Olympics.''

''What happened to him?''

The blissful smile faded fast. ''He dumped me for a former Miss Minnesota. Think blond, Swedish, you'd want to kill her.''

''But you're gorgeous.''

''Thanks, but she was gorgeouser. The bastard. He'd made me look beyond the surface to the man inside, and he dumped me for a twinkie.''

''So I'm not looking for a bald, short, funny guy with amazing tongue control.''

''Ah, go out with whoever you like. Just buy a vibrator, so you'll always have a love you can depend on.''

YAWNING and thinking she'd get to bed early, Shari was still thinking about Therese's theory of men when she got home. She checked her mail in the lobby, and winced. Two letters to her downstairs neighbor. Suddenly, the dyslexic postie wasn't quite so charming.

Unfortunately, her apartment building had security boxes, so she couldn't slip the letters in the correct mailbox. She could leave them on the console table in the foyer, but it didn't seem quite right. Luke hadn't done anything wrong, he'd merely embarrassed them both.

She picked up his mail along with her own. Maybe she could slip the letters under his door in the dead of night.

But when she got to her floor, puffing slightly from running up two flights of stairs, a familiar shape hovered outside her door.

She started to blush, and wanted to kick herself for being such a fool. So he read a how-to book. Good for him.

He turned as she approached and, in spite of her new knowledge, her knees still went weak. The eyes, the smile, the dimple... Could an Olympic-gold-medal tongue really compete with all that?

"Hi," he said. He didn't seem embarrassed, so she decided she wouldn't be, either.

"Hi." She halted outside her apartment and sorted through the letters in her hand, handing him his two.

"Thanks. These are for you." She took the bundle from his outstretched hand, *not* thinking about the last time they'd done this. It was the furthest thing from her mind.

"Um, sorry about last time," he said.

He had to bring it up. No wonder he was a dud in bed if his social graces were any indication. What was

the appropriate response here? *Hope you get it right?*
Let me know if you need help with your homework?

She still hadn't recovered from the discovery that
her fantasy hunk had turned out to be a limp noodle
in the sex department. Gosh, speaking of limp noodles, maybe he had some kind of…physical problem.
She'd heard of men who simply got shortchanged in
the…um, equipment. Had that happened to him?

Her eyes focused on his crotch. Before she caught
herself, she gave a soundless gasp and glanced up
again, ascertaining that this did not in fact appear to
be his problem. A respectable bulge nestled in the
crotch of his jeans.

She caught a sparkle in his eyes she could have
sworn was amusement. He thought this was funny?

In any case, size didn't matter half as much as what
a man did with his equipment. Maybe he couldn't do
much of anything. Maybe he needed medication or
that penis pump she'd read about that helped a man
sustain an erection. Her gaze dropped once again to
his crotch. Did it need to get pumped up before it
could party?

"It all works, if that's what's worrying you," he
assured her.

This time her gasp was audible. She glanced up
and down the hallway, ensuring it was empty.
"Your…your works are none of my business."

"I know," he said, taking a step closer. His voice
dropped to a deliciously husky murmur. "I was hoping we could change that."

"I beg your pardon?" she said in her teacher-to-
bad-student voice. She had this tone perfected. It
worked on male students who tried to tell her dirty

jokes, forgot themselves and used bad language, or made lewd comments within her hearing. There was a matching look that went with the tone. She would pull up through the neck and retract her head so she could look down her nose at the culprit.

It made swaggering sophomores cringe every time.

All it did with Luke was deepen the amusement crinkling his eyes. "There's something I want to ask you. It sort of concerns the other night."

Halfway down the corridor a door started to open. It was the garrulous and nosy Mr. Forrester. If he caught her in the hallway with Luke she'd never hear the end of it.

Shoving her key in the lock, she opened the door, and all but shoved Luke inside. "Let's talk in here," she said. "Better without an audience."

"Sure. Thanks." He walked down the small hallway, right into the living area. "It's nice." He gestured to the mishmash of furniture she'd collected and prettied up with embroidered cushions and colorful throws. "Exactly like mine, only classier."

"Thank you. Would you like to sit down?" Oh, Lord. She should have put up with nosy Mr. Forrester and kept Luke in the hallway. Inviting him in was only encouraging him. Plus, it made her feel as though she were entertaining and had to be polite.

"Yes." He sat in the overstuffed floral-chintz sofa and she chose the opposite chair.

Luke glanced at her and then at the mail in his hands as though he'd forgotten it was there. He put his letters down on the coffee table then leaned back, legs slightly parted, hands on thighs. Relaxed, confident. Too gorgeous for her peace of mind.

Even though she knew his secret, her body didn't seem to have caught on to it. She felt the same potent pull of attraction, the same melting desire. It wasn't fair. Probably her inappropriate lust was just a symptom that she'd been without a boyfriend too long.

She tossed her own mail down, where it made a messy fan. A couple of bills and a creamy vellum envelope that had wedding invitation written all over it. She cringed inside. The flu wasn't as contagious as the wedding bug that had bitten so many of her approaching-thirty friends.

It wasn't that she grudged any of her friends or acquaintances happiness, it was just that she was starting to wonder if she'd be attending their silver and golden wedding anniversaries—still alone.

Given the appalling way she'd been misjudging men lately, it seemed eminently possible that she'd be spending her whole life single.

She squinted at the return address on the invitation and felt herself pale.

"Oh, no," she moaned aloud.

"What's the matter?"

The voice startled her and she glanced up. In the shock of seeing that wedding invite, she'd forgotten he was there. "B. J. McLaren's getting married."

"I see. My condolences." She caught the amusement again, crinkling the edges of his eyes. It made her want to smile back, except she was too mad at B.J.

"She was one of my best friends, then she stole my boyfriend in college." The hurt pride, which had never entirely healed, throbbed again as she saw the two of them smooching in the library. "Walt Whitman introduced them."

"From the great beyond?"

She shook her head. "They took a unit of American poetry together and claim they fell in love during *Leaves of Grass.*"

"Where were you?"

"Milton. *Paradise Lost.* I haven't seen B.J. in…it must be three or four years. Now she's marrying him and wants to shove my nose in it one more time."

"What a bitch."

She chuckled. "My sentiments exactly." She opened the expensive envelope and withdrew the card. "'Request the honor of your presence…blah, blah, blah. Oh, and here's a handwritten note at the bottom. 'Please bring your significant other. Randy and I would love to see you both.'"

"Sounds like she's trying to mend fences."

"Sounds like she found out I'm single, and wants to make me feel like the last unattached loser in America." As if Shari needed the reminder. Maybe the marriage flu bug had caught her, too, but she was ready to settle down. She had a great career, loved living in Seattle, her ovaries were young and efficient. She was a woman in her prime mating and child-bearing years. All she needed was the right man. Where the hell was he?

Luke shrugged. "So don't go."

Her jaw dropped, her attention snagged from a mental review of her wardrobe. "Not go? I have to go. This—" she flapped the pale cream, engraved invitation at him "—is a slap in the face, a challenge to mortal combat. Oh, no. I'm going."

She checked the date of the wedding. A month away. "I've got four weeks to prepare," she said, only vaguely aware that she was speaking aloud to a virtual stranger. "I'll need a great dress, a great date—" She dropped her hand to her stomach and tested the muscle tone. "An intense fitness regimen. Maybe cut back on fats and try to lose a couple of pounds."

She glanced at her watch. If she could get rid of Luke, she could drop to the carpet and do some abdominal crunches and push-ups right away. With only a month to prepare, she didn't have a moment to lose.

The sad truth was, she'd never entirely recovered from the humiliation of losing Randy to B.J. back in their senior year. She hadn't exactly been shy about wearing her broken heart on her sleeve, either. All her old college friends probably still thought of her as a poor pathetic loser who couldn't hang on to her boyfriend.

B.J. wanted to go another round? Shari was more than ready. She was older, smarter, and a lot better at handling her emotions. She had a good job and a life she liked.

This was her chance to prove it. She needed a fabulous dress, new accessories. She groaned mentally. The most important accessory she needed wasn't a new purse or high heels. It was a gorgeous hunk of testosterone hanging off her arm. Where was she going to find one of those?

With only a month to go, she couldn't afford to waste a minute. She snapped her attention back to Luke. The quicker she got rid of him and started on her master plan, the better. "You wanted to talk to me about something?"

"Shari, I need your help."

She paused, while she tried to forget about B.J., the boyfriend thief.

"You need my help with what?"

"You know that book you saw? *Sex for Total Morons*?"

"Yes." Blushing was childish and embarrassing. She would not blush.

"It's kind of for couples."

She forgot all about the heat creeping into her cheeks and felt her eyes widen. "You mean, total morons pair up?"

He grinned. "It's not that, exactly. The book is separated into chapters…and there are lessons and, um, exercises. I need someone to practice with. Since you're the only woman who knows about the book, I wondered if you'd do them with me."

She jumped to her feet, all thoughts of B.J., orange blossoms and "Ave Maria" flying out of her head. She could not believe this man. "You're asking me to have sex with you? Maybe you should grab yourself a copy of *Polite Conversation for Total Morons*. I'll give you a hint. We are not having one."

She stalked to the door. What kind of sick game was this creep playing with her? No wonder he couldn't get laid.

"No, wait." He rose and followed her. "You misunderstood me. I'm not asking for sex. Just some compassion. You seem like a person with a good heart."

"I also have a brain bigger than a pea." With a jerk, she opened the door and glared at him. "Out."

"There's nothing but kissing until Chapter Four."

"Tell someone who cares."

"I didn't put that well. I'm sorry. Look." He ran a hand through his already disheveled hair, looking little-boy lost and adorable. "The women I meet, they have…preconceived notions about me. They expect…certain things. But you, you're different. You don't see me that way at all. I thought maybe you'd help me. Just to get started. The first few chapters. I promise we wouldn't do anything you didn't feel completely comfortable with."

Once again she wondered how someone so gorgeous could be such a dud under the blankets. One of life's unsolved mysteries. "You're asking me to sleep with you out of pity?"

He made a gesture of dismissal with his hand. "Forget about sex. I just want to see if the book works. If you'd practice the first couple of chapters with me, say, every Friday night, I'd be really grateful."

She was ready with an unqualified no. A "Hell, no" so firm he'd never darken her doorway again. But her attention was caught by the invitation still clutched in her hand. Instead of no she stared at Luke as a brilliant, fully formed notion popped into her head.

She narrowed her eyes at him. Apart from the little problem no one else needed to know about, he was better-looking than anybody else she was likely to dig up in one short month. If she kept him on a tight rein and didn't let him talk much, he could pass as a major find in the boyfriend department.

"You said there was nothing but kissing until chapter four, right?"

A grin of pure hope lit his face. "Right."

"I'll make you a deal. I'll go to chapter four with you if you go to B.J. and Randy's wedding with me."

The grin vanished, replaced by an expression of revulsion. "You want me to go to this cheesy wedding as your date?"

"No. I want you to go to this cheesy wedding as my devoted love slave."

3

"LOVE SLAVE?" Luke couldn't believe she'd just used that term. Was she a kinky, black-leather dominatrix once the lights went down?

Oh, man. He didn't mind a woman dominating him once in a while—in fact, it was a total turn-on when a lady called the shots. But he liked his turn in control, too.

If she was of the leather and whips persuasion, he respected her right to her pleasure. He just didn't share that particular taste.

She must have caught some of his thoughts, for she pinkened. "I didn't mean *love slave* in any kind of pervy way. I mean, I want you to act like that at the wedding. As if I'm the most fascinating, intelligent, gorgeous woman around."

"Sexy, too," he added, thinking that was one of her greatest charms.

"Well, yes, of course. Sexy, too. While we're at the wedding you won't even look at another woman, you'll pretend to be completely smitten with me."

He could see her enthusiasm building as she outlined his role for him. Her sparkly chocolate-brown eyes lit up with excitement, her whole body radiated purpose and energy—he could easily imagine himself half crazy about her. "Shouldn't be too tough to pull off,'' he assured her, grinning when the pink in her cheeks deepened at the compliment.

When he'd first met her, he hadn't pegged her for the blushing type, but those cheeks bloomed roses at the slightest provocation. He wondered if they flushed like that when she was aroused. He wondered if he'd ever get the chance to find out.

''Well, thanks,'' she said.

''So we've got four weeks to get me in shape for the big day.''

''That's right. I'm talking tuxedo, hairstyle, the full deal.''

Tuxedo was a word that just plain made him twitchy. Tuxedo meant weddings, which he hated, and usually, another walk down the aisle for dear old dad. Luke had finally cracked and bought himself a tux that fit properly. Besides, it was cheaper in the long run than renting, the way his father kept getting married. Still, if sticking himself in a monkey suit and tossing rice around was the price to pay for Shari's cooperation with his book, he'd pay it—and make sure she followed through on her part of the bargain.

''And a month means we can do a chapter a week. We'll learn about each other. Four weeks from now, we'll be able to fool anyone that I'm your devoted love slave.''

''A week for every chapter, huh?'' She stepped back and crossed her arms under her breasts. ''I don't know. I think I'm having second thoughts.'' She stared at his mouth as though trying to decide how she felt about kissing him. If she stared at his lips much longer, she was going to find out.

''Well, I'm not thrilled about dressing in a monkey

suit to watch a couple who dissed you in college get hitched.'' He shrugged, knowing this was his moment of truth. ''Your call.''

She glared at him, then down at the invitation waded in her hand. ''Oh, all right. But just to chapter four. Kissing is my limit.'' Then she opened the door and made scooting motions with her hands. ''I have to do some sit-ups.''

He stopped at the doorway and gazed into eyes already sparkling with the light of battle. Look out B.J. and look out Luke. ''I don't think you need sit-ups. Your body looks perfect to me.''

Their gazes caught and held and her lips parted in an unconscious offering. He had to restrain himself from leaning in to kiss her. She was adorable, sexy and delicious. Why was she stressing about co-ed heartbreak? ''I think you had a lucky escape. Any dork who'd dump you deserves to spend the rest of his life with B.J.''

She laughed shakily. ''I think there's a compliment in there somewhere.''

''Sure is. Night.''

He waited until Shari's door shut behind him and he was back in the deserted corridor before he leaped in the air and pumped his fist. *Yes, yes, yes!*

She'd gone for it. Shari, the babe of his apartment block, had agreed to work through the first four chapters of *Sex for Total Morons*. And he hadn't lied to get her help. He hadn't even stretched the truth. All he'd done was ask her to work through the exercises in the book with him. He hadn't said he needed the lessons. If she made assumptions, that was her problem.

Of course there was a price to be paid. He wasn't a big fan of weddings at the best of times. Having attended all four of his father's—although admittedly he'd attended the first in utero, so he couldn't be expected to remember it—he'd developed a cynic's aversion to the whole ceremony.

On one point he was determined—no woman was dragging him up the aisle. No rice showers for Luke. Free and single suited him fine.

If his dad had kept his brain in his head instead of his pants, he might have figured out the same thing. Some men weren't cut out for commitment or settling down with one woman. Some men needed the excitement of new partners and the adventure of the chase.

His father was one of those men. He never should have married.

Luke was his father's son in that regard. But he was smart enough not to fall into the velvet trap of marriage and then spend the next few years gnawing off his own foot to escape, littering bitter ex-wives and lonely children in his wake.

Luke liked and respected women too much ever to commit to one. He was always up-front about that, so there were few tears and tantrums in his love life. Not a lot of deep meaning, either, but about that he was philosophical: you can't have everything.

There were twelve chapters in Lance's masterpiece. Shari had committed to a month, one chapter a week. Of course, if the book was worth the paper it was printed on, four weeks of seduction ought to ease her into chapter five as smoothly as a man eases an eager woman onto silk sheets.

Yep, he foresaw twelve passion-filled weeks stretching ahead of him. That was almost three months. A nice run of time, about the time it usually took for him to start feeling the first twinges of boredom.

As long as he was clear, there'd be no hard feelings. She'd get a date for the wedding from hell, he'd find out if the book really worked, and they'd both have some healthy adult fun.

It was a terrific plan.

What could possibly go wrong?

"ARE YOU COMPLETELY insane?" Therese's forehead was creased, her eyes bugged and her mouth gaped.

They'd ducked into the female staff washroom for a hurried conversation between classes. Shari'd been so eager to spill her news she couldn't wait until after school.

"You look surprised. I thought you'd be thrilled."

"Thrilled about you playing love doctor with some guy you don't even know?"

Therese checked her reflection in the scratched mirror and hauled out her cosmetic bag. She dipped a finger into a little plastic pot, smearing glossy pink goo onto her full lips. A hint of strawberry scented the air, and Shari shook her head. It was the kind of cosmetic the students used. Somehow it worked on Therese—the hip, young clothes, funky hair and strawberry-scented lip gloss.

"Does that stuff taste like strawberries, too?"

Therese touched her pink tongue to her full upper lip and nodded. "Yeah, it does. Want some?"

"No, thanks. I want to know why you don't think this is a good idea. He's not short, bald or fat. He's gorgeous. If I help him get started on the path to becoming a great lover, I'll have helped all woman-kind.''

Therese just rolled her eyes and pulled out a pink plastic brush. As she dragged it through her glossy black hair, she glared at Shari from the mirror. "First, how old is he?''

She shrugged. "Maybe thirty?''

"When did he first start having sex?''

"I don't know.''

"I'll bet he's had ten to fifteen years of practice, and he still can't get it right. I mean, come on. I've been playing the saxophone for that long. Do you ever hear me play a wrong note?''

Not only was Therese a talented amateur, but she'd earned her living as a musician in Montreal and Paris before deciding to become a teacher. "No. You never play a wrong note. But you had to learn how.''

"Hon, some kids have a tin ear. They are never going to play an instrument without making you cringe. Some people can't dance. Some can't play sports...'' She shrugged.

"And some are never going to make it as lovers. Is that your point?''

Therese put her brush away and zipped her bag. "I'm saying, he's had a lot of years to get it right.''

"My mother went back to university at sixty to take the history degree she always wanted.'' The school bell shrilled, echoing off the dull green tiles on the wall, letting them know they had to hustle to class. "She's carrying a four-point average,'' Shari said as she pulled open the door and held it for her friend.

"We aren't talking history."

"I think you can improve at anything if you're willing to work at it."

"Fifty bucks says you don't last out the month."

As they joined the milling crowd of teens headed for classes, Shari whispered, "Done. Fifty it is."

Of course, Therese didn't know this was just a side bet. Shari already had one major deal going with Luke. If she didn't need a spectacular specimen of manhood—at least on the outside—as her date for B.J.'s wedding, well, maybe she wouldn't have jumped at the opportunity to take on some one-on-one tutoring at night.

Although, she thought as she entered her classroom, it was kind of flattering that Luke had chosen her to be his teacher. He must see her as a sensual woman of experience.

She grinned smugly to herself. Maybe she wasn't a virtuoso of the saxophone, but she had hidden talents. She had to admit, Luke could have chosen a lot worse.

The usual start-of-class shuffling and noise greeted her. She stowed her bag in the drawer of the scarred oak desk, took a deep breath and intoned in a strong, clear voice, "'Death be not proud!'"

Silence fell with gratifying speed. All butts found their assigned seats and thirty teenagers faced her with varying degrees of enthusiasm.

She let her gaze scan the class. "'Death be not proud!'" She pointed to a figure slouched in one of the back seats, staring at the floor. Somebody hadn't done his homework. "Dylan, give me the rest of the first stanza of Donne's poem, please."

John Donne would not have been proud had he been privileged to hear the way his poetry was butchered. Still, it was something to have youngsters learning your verses centuries after you wrote them. Perhaps he would be proud.

Shari loved poetry, but she was ready to take a break from hearing it punctuated by ums and ahs, read in voices cracking with adolescence, stuttered over, mispronounced. Still, bless their hearts, they tried. Her next unit would be a relief for everybody. The curriculum specified a short stint on journalism. Maybe she'd even dig up a working reporter as a guest.

She was still thinking about that when she arrived home, a bag of groceries—mostly veggies and low-cal yogurt—in hand, and a satchetful of marking.

The phone was ringing. She struggled with her key, the grocery bag banging against her legs as she let herself into her apartment and ran for the phone. Every muscle protested. Maybe she shouldn't have worked out quite so hard after school.

She caught it just before the answering service. "Hello?"

"Did I catch you in the middle of something?" The deep, rich voice, lightly threaded with humor, got her heart pounding. It was familiar, tantalizing her like a spice she'd tasted but couldn't identify.

"No, I just got home." If she kept him talking for a few more seconds she'd figure out who he was. How hard could it be? Not many men in her life sounded so drop-dead sexy.

"I was just calling to make a date," he said.

Date. Date? Who was she dating?

"Date?"

"For chapter one."

"Chapter one. Right." *Luke*. Her breathlessness didn't abate. If anything, it worsened. "I, um, didn't realize we'd be starting so soon."

"I'm eager to begin. I thought maybe this Friday night, if you're not already busy."

"Friday night? Um." She knew damned well she wasn't busy Friday night. She and Therese sometimes went out after work, but her friend was going away for the weekend, and Shari hadn't made any plans. Still, was she ready for *Sex for Total Morons*? She shrugged; she was as ready as she'd ever be. Might as well get on with it. "Sure. Friday's fine."

"Wonderful." His voice was warm and full of implied goodies. She pictured him talking to her from a floor below and smiled at the floor on the left hand side of the living room, where, she assumed, they shared a wall. "Why don't you come down around seven?"

"Oh, we're doing this at your place?" Suddenly she wasn't so sure. "I thought maybe we'd do it at my apartment."

"Well, why don't we take turns? This week my apartment, next week yours?"

"I guess so. That sounds fair." In fact the whole thing sounded horrendous and she couldn't help thinking that this was all B. J. McLaren's fault. Shari had left college and its bad memories. Why was the woman still messing with her love life?

"Great. I'll see you Friday."

A thought struck her. "Luke?"

"Yes?"

"What's in chapter one?"

He laughed softly. "You'll find out Friday."

Even though he couldn't see her, she narrowed her eyes in a don't-mess-with-me-mister expression. "Nothing beyond kissing, right?"

"That's right. There's nothing but kissing until chapter five."

"All right. See you Friday."

LUKE CONTEMPLATED the candles he'd purchased. In his experience, women liked them. Candlelight helped camouflage figure faults he could never see but his women friends so often swore they had. Whatever.

Would that be cheating, though? He was trying to see if his book worked. He didn't want to jeopardize the pure science of his findings by adding a lot of seductive extras. Candlelight, wine, flowers...all the usual stuff might be considered cheating.

And yet no man could be expected to seduce a woman over milk and cookies with all the lights on. Well, come to think of it, he'd done that in high school with his first girlfriend. For a long time after that, just the sight of cinnamon-swirl cookies gave him a hard-on.

Had he mentioned wine and candlelight in chapter one? If so, he was off the hook. What the hell had he written, anyway?

Irritated, and vaguely nervous about the upcoming "lesson," he opened the book and started reading.

Seduction begins, not with the body, but with the mind.

He nodded. "Smart fellow, Lance."

Conversation is foreplay. If you can make the man or woman you are interested in feel desired, they'll reciprocate and develop a heightened interest in you. And this is where you, the Total Moron, stop being seen as a TM and become a possible bed buddy. This whole book is about your journey from TM to Outstanding Lover.

He skipped through all the rest of the intro to locate the first exercise specifically for men. Ah, there it was.

Are you ready? Let's go.

Exercise One.

Go to a crowded bar. If you're on your own, try to pick out a woman who looks friendly. If you have a partner, and you both feel you need this book, I suggest you go back to the beginning of your relationship and start over. I don't care if you have three kids—pretend you're meeting for the first time.

Look your woman full in the eyes. The Dallas Cowboys' cheerleaders can walk by naked. Focus your attention on this person you are "meeting" for the first time. Ask her what she did today. Ask her about her job, her interests.

Watch her body language. Is she inviting you closer? Sending you messages with her eyes?

Go with the flow. If you can get away with a quick touch on the shoulder, do it. An accidental brushing of your arm against hers is always a turn-on. But don't overdo it. You're not taking lint off a suit here. And use a light touch. If you knock her off her bar stool, notch it down for next time.

When it comes time to leave, walk her to her car, the bus, a taxi, whatever. Now, you're dying to kiss her, right? Just get in there and clean her tonsils?

Don't do it.

Take her hand. Tell her you had a great time. Try to get her number or give her yours.

Leave her wanting more. This, my comrades in the trenches, is the secret. Leave them wanting more.

Now, if the moment feels right, brush your lips across her cheek. Look right into her eyes and tell her you'll call.

Luke dropped the book.

Damn. He'd forgotten that. The first exercise took place out on the town.

So much for candles. He checked his watch. Shari was supposed to be here in half an hour. He found her number and called.

"Hello?" Her voice sounded huskier on the phone. Sexy as hell.

"Hey, I just read chapter one. We're supposed to meet in a bar and talk."

There was a moment of silence. "What kind of a bar?"

"The book doesn't say."

"You're supposed to go to a bar to seduce a woman. That's the first lesson?"

"I guess."

She sighed. "That book has to have been written by a man."

There wasn't a whole lot he could say to that. "Just give it a try, okay?"

"I'm not much of a bar person. Where do you want to meet?"

He thought about it. Not his local joint, too many people knew him there. Besides, it wasn't classy enough for Shari. He searched his mind and came up with a bistro/bar in a hotel not too far from them. On Fridays there was live music of the piano-and-quartet variety. It was quiet enough to talk, but also had a pretty good crowd of single professionals. She'd probably love it.

"The Rainbow Room. Do you know it?"

"Yes."

"Can you get there, say, around seven? I'll arrive a little later. You have to pretend you don't know me. We're meeting for the first time."

"This is the silliest thing I've ever heard."

Luke grit his teeth. Truth was, he agreed with her. When he'd written that tripe in chapter one, he'd never imagined himself traipsing off to a bar to pick up a woman who lived one floor above him. He sensed her wavering on the whole thing and decided to remind her that this bargain went both ways. "I dropped my tux off at the dry cleaner's today, just to make sure it's nice and crisp for that wedding."

"Don't get to the bar too late or somebody else will get lesson one."

He chuckled at her cocky tone. Somehow, he had a feeling this evening was going to be fun. He just

had to remember to follow his own instructions to the
letter. *No improvising*.

If he wasn't trying so hard to play this charade
strictly by the book, he'd be tempted to toy with her
on the phone. She had a quick wit and wasn't afraid
to put him in his place. He imagined there weren't
many subjects about which she didn't know something. But for his experiment to have any validity, he
had to stay within the guidelines of the book. Flirtation by phone before he even got to chapter one didn't
suit his notions of fair play. So he squelched his desire
to have some telephone fun and told her he'd arrive
a few minutes after her.

"And, Luke," she said in that snotty teacher's
voice that completely turned him on, "next time, I'll
expect you to do your homework ahead of time."

4

OF ALL THE CRAZY, ridiculous ideas. Shari made herself stare at the wedding invite in all its grisly embossed-silver-roses glory. This ghastly evening pretending to be picked up in a bar by a man she wasn't at all certain she wanted anything to do with was B.J.'s fault. As if the woman hadn't tortured her enough in college, she'd followed Shari into the rest of her life just to screw that up for her, too.

Grumbling, she hauled on a skirt and a red clinging top. After all, she reasoned, no need for Luke to have it easy with her dressed as a little brown mouse hiding in the corner. With luck, he'd actually have to put a bit of effort into this absurd faux pick-up routine.

With that in mind, she outlined her full lips in a nice deep mulberry shade and added an extra layer of mascara.

War paint in place, she was on her way.

By the time she got to the hotel, she was feeling a little ticked. What was she? Some kind of prop to be used so he could act out the part of Luke the Seducer in his own private show?

Shari wasn't at all the passive type. She lifted her chin. Luke might as well find out that the road out of Total Moronism wasn't as easy as reading a few chapters in a book.

Women liked to star in their own stories, as Luke Lawson was about to learn.

She walked into the dimly lit Rainbow Room and glanced around. It was fairly busy with an after-work, predinner and theater crowd. All the good tables were taken, but there were a couple of empty tables in the middle and a few vacant stools at the bar.

It would be so easy to take a seat at an empty table and wait for her "date" to pick her up.

She strolled past the tables, made her way to the back and settled herself on a bar stool. The bartender tossed her a grin from where he was pulling a beer. "Be right with you."

She returned the smile. "Thanks."

It gave her a moment or two to decide what to drink, but by the time the bartender stood in front of her, she still didn't know. She wrinkled her nose in indecision. "White wine?"

The bartender shook his head and leaned close. "Not for a lady in red."

Damn, he was flirting with her. Her plan was already working. Was she good or what?

She twinkled back at him. "What do you suggest?"

He leaned his elbows on the wooden counter, just an inch closer than necessary, and studied her. "I'm thinking exotic but cool. Maybe a little spicy with a touch of salt. And I happen to make the best margarita this side of Mexico City."

She giggled. He was cute. Probably a couple of years younger than she, but he definitely had attitude and was obviously only too happy to while away a few minutes between customers flirting with the only lone woman in the vicinity. "A margarita sounds perfect. Thanks."

He turned her drink into a performance complete with swagger and bravado, and she enjoyed every second of it. When the drink arrived, it was perfect. Cool, salt-sweet and tangy. She surfaced from the first shivery sip and nodded her approval.

"What's your name?" he asked, wiping the dark bar in front of her with a towel, although it looked perfectly clean to her.

"Shari. What's yours?"

"Les. I don't remember seeing you here before."

"I don't come here that often." She'd dated an engineer a couple of times and they'd dropped by after a night at the theater, she remembered. But that had been more than a year ago. In fact, since she'd broken up with the perfectly nice but unexciting Peter six months ago, she hadn't been to very many places like this.

"What brings you here tonight? Meeting someone?" He let her see the light of interest in his eyes.

"Yes, she's meeting someone," said a deep and somewhat annoyed voice from behind her.

She turned her head to find Luke wearing a possessive scowl.

"And who might that be?" she asked. According to chapter one, they were supposed to be strangers, after all.

"Me." He must have forgotten he was supposed to play a stranger. She'd rattled him out of his textbook exercise already and, luckily for him, that made her feel charitable.

"You know this guy?" her new friend Les asked,

ready, she was certain, to have Luke thrown out on his arrogant ass.

However, she needed a date for B.J.'s wedding and somehow she didn't think getting Luke tossed into a back alley was going to improve his role as her devoted love slave.

"Yes," she said. "I know him."

Luke glanced to either side of her, but both stools were occupied. "Could we move to a table?" he asked her.

"Sure."

She reached for her drink, but the bartender stopped her with a hand on hers. "I'll bring your drink over for you, Shari." She almost laughed at the deliberate way he used her name in front of Luke. Oh, yeah. She'd made her point. The bartender turned his attention to Luke. "What can I get you?"

"A pint of whatever you have on tap."

"Coming right up."

They made their way to an empty table and settled themselves. Although there were waitstaff, the bartender brought their drinks over himself. He placed Shari's drink in front of her, a large frosty mug of ale in front of Luke and a black plastic bowl of nuts in the middle of the table. "There you go, Shari," he said with the ghost of a wink.

"Thanks, Les," she said, enjoying chapter one much more than she'd thought she would.

"Yes, thanks, *Les,*" her date said.

"No problem, man," he said.

Luke lifted his beer in her direction, then drank deeply. She followed suit, sipping her own drink.

"I hope I didn't horn in on anything," he said when he'd swallowed.

"Pardon? Oh, you mean the bartender. No. Not at all. He was just being friendly to a woman alone."

He glanced at her, a devilish gleam in his deep green eyes. "Do I need to apologize?"

"No." She allowed herself a tiny, self-satisfied smirk. "I think I've made my point. So, now what do we do?"

"Hell if I know," he said, slumping back in his armchair. "You've completely thrown me off my agenda."

She nodded, pleased. "That's good. I think being spontaneous is more fun."

He leaned closer, his gaze never leaving hers. "Then, can I be completely spontaneous and tell you you look good enough to eat?" He reached over and ran his index finger up her arm and over her shoulder, coming to rest lightly at the juncture of shoulder and throat.

She shivered at the contact of his finger, cold from the beer mug, on the naked flesh of her shoulder. "Is that in chapter one?" she asked, feeling bereft when he put his arm back at his side.

"Yes."

"What else is in chapter one?"

He was wearing a navy polo shirt. At least, she thought it was navy; it appeared black in the dim light. It molded to his chest and she saw the muscles of his arms shift the fabric every time he moved. A trio of piano, bass and drums played softly in the background.

He leaned closer and stared right into her eyes. It

felt as personal as a kiss. "We talk about you all night," he said.

O-oh, something about the way he said those words made them feel like a caress. She shifted on her chair and gazed right back at him. His lips were nice, she thought. Full without being punched-in-the-mouth puffy, and firm. Darkness pooled in the cleft in his chin.

"We talk about me. Okay. I can do that. Then what?"

"Then we go home."

Of course. She wasn't sure when the kissing part took place in the book. If that didn't happen until chapter four, she wondered what they'd do for the next three weeks. At the pace of this book, Total Morons would be into their golden years before they saw any action.

"So," he said, half joking. "Tell me about yourself."

"I'm a Capricorn," she said in a bright, ditzy voice. "I like considerate people and I hate guys who smoke."

"Come on, help me out here, will you?"

"I couldn't help myself. Okay, ask me something specific."

"What do you like most about being a teacher?"

"Bringing poetry alive." She was surprised she'd even said that. But she was even more surprised that he'd remembered her profession when she'd only mentioned it casually during one of their exchanging-mail chitchat sessions. How odd to admit her passion to a virtual stranger. Still, he'd asked and was gazing at her as though he were truly interested, so she continued.

"Kids don't get a lot of poetry in their lives. I love it when you suddenly see that a student gets it. They'll be stuttering along and then it's as though the rhythms and the beauty of the language catch them unaware. Those are my breakthrough moments. They don't happen often, but no one leaves my class without a nodding acquaintance with Shakespeare, Wordsworth…" She glanced at him with a wry grin. "Even Whitman. Right now we're studying John Donne."

"'No man is an island.' Good choice for teenagers."

"That's the very poem we discussed in class today." She chuckled softly and told Luke that when the bell to change classes had rung, Terry, a smart but lazy junior had intoned in a deep baritone, "'Never send to know for whom the bell tolls; it tolls for thee.'"

Class anecdotes were safe and gave the illusion of talking about her, while in fact she shared little personal information.

They were into their second drink when he said, "You're single." It wasn't a question but a statement, and yet she felt as though he really wanted to know.

"Yes. I'm single."

Luke reached forward and played with the fingers of her left hand. "Still pining over Randy?"

She was impressed he remembered the guy's name. "No. Of course not. I'm between men, that's all."

"How long's it been?"

"Six months." She didn't know why she should feel defensive. She hadn't met anyone she cared for enough to get serious with in half a year. So what? "How about you?"

He shook his head. "Tonight's only about you."

"I was with someone for a year or so, but it wasn't going anywhere. I'm getting to a stage in my life where I'd rather be alone than with someone who bores me."

"I'll try not to bore you in our four weeks together," he said softly.

"I'd appreciate that," she said, thinking that bored was not how she felt about the way he was toying with her fingers. The man must have memorized a diagram in chapter one.

The expression in those mossy green eyes went way past chapter four. His gaze communicated wanting, promised intimacy. Every womanly atom in her body was answering his unspoken question, *Yes, yes, yes!* She forced herself to swallow. *Down, girl.*

She stared again at his lips, wetted her own with her tongue and then said an incredibly stupid thing before she could stop herself. "When do we kiss?"

He grinned at her, his teeth gleaming white in the darkness. "Let's leave that for a surprise."

He'd taste like beer and hot male. Were his lips as firm as they looked? Would he have a clue what to do with them? At least let him be a good kisser.

"You know," she said, in what she hoped was a reasonable teacher's tone, "I think we should give the kissing a try quite soon. Just in case."

"In case what?"

She shrugged. "We might really have to work at it. Don't forget, we only have a month." She watched a line of condensation form near the top of his beer mug. "Maybe I should go get a copy of that book."

The moisture on his mug wavered as his arm jerked, jarring the glass mug. "No," he all but shouted. "Don't do that."

"Why not?"

"Then you'll know…"

A quiver of amusement shook her. "Know all your secrets?"

"Yeah. And you'll know all my moves before I make them. It wouldn't be fair."

"I thought you said this book was for couples? Isn't there a section for women?"

He stuck out his lower lip like a pouting child and puffed out a breath that lifted the lock of hair that had fallen onto his forehead. He brushed it back irritably.

"Yes. There's a section for women. And maybe we'll get to that. But for now, could we please do this my way?"

She shifted irritably in her seat, wishing she wasn't so wildly attracted to this man. And if she had to tutor him in seducing a woman, she'd at least like to do it on her own terms and with her own agenda, not according to some self-proclaimed sex expert's idea of how to go about it. "He's got some nerve, this Lance person."

"Why do you say that?"

"Imagine a man writing a book for couples. How does he know how women think? What they want? What…"

"Turns them on?" His voice taunted her.

"Exactly."

He shrugged. "Maybe he's asked them."

Thinking about her conversation with Therese, she snorted. "Not if he's a flesh-and-blood man." She scanned the crowd, smiled a little at a couple slow dancing on the small square of parquet dance floor. "This place is getting busy."

"What did you mean?"

She glanced at him in surprise. "More people are arriving than are leaving. Not so unusual for a Friday night."

He jerked his head in quick denial. "Not that. The thing you said before, about men not asking women what they want."

He appeared a bit huffy at her assertion, and she hid her smile behind her drink, sipping from the cool, salt-rimmed glass, thinking the bartender had known what she wanted.

"I'm saying they don't ask women what they want. Men make assumptions. A guy who calls himself Lance Flagstaff is a perfect example."

"A man can't help his own name." He was reddening, she could see it even in the dim light of the bar. He must have a really grim love life if he'd invested this heavily in the theories of some dumb book. And speaking of dumb...

"Lance Flagstaff has to be a pseudonym. Any writer who'd choose it must be in love with his own lance."

"Maybe it's a woman."

"What?" she asked on a surprised giggle.

"If it's a fake name, it could be a woman writing that book. Or a couple."

She thought for a second. "As a kind of joke, you mean?"

"Why not?"

She recalled seeing Mr. Flagstaff's byline in a national women's mag she sometimes purchased with her groceries. He gave the male perspective on dating and sex. He also answered questions from readers.

"I'm pretty sure he's a guy. That's not a pen name a woman or a couple would choose."

"Want another drink?" He gestured to her nearly empty glass.

Did she? She wasn't sure. In fact, she wasn't sure how she felt about this whole thing. Knowing he was following a book she hadn't read left her feeling off kilter. "What else is on tonight's agenda?"

"What agenda?" His eyes were focused on her lower lip.

She waved her hands around to indicate the bar. "Do we stay here? Go somewhere else? Go home? What else does it say in chapter one?"

His gaze never wavered. "Kissing is optional."

"Pardon?"

"That's what it says in chapter one. Kissing is optional."

"Oh." She gulped, wondering how she felt about her options. And about this very strange date.

But she had to remember she had her own agenda, which was the only reason she'd agreed to this crazy plan in the first place.

"Do you want another?" she asked, stalling for time, trying to decide what she did want.

"Another what?" She'd never known a man who could stay so focused on her, despite the noise of their surroundings, the comings and goings, the women strutting by them. He wasn't glancing around every five minutes to see if there was someone he knew or someone he'd like to get to know. He made her feel that she was the most interesting woman in the room. And, whether or not he'd picked up the tip in some ridiculous book, she found it flattering. And unusual.

"Drink."

"No. Let's get out of here."

She nodded. "I kind of overdid my workout today. I think I need an early night."

When they hit the parking lot, the quiet struck her. Her ears still seemed to pulse with the sultry jazz and the talk and laughter of the Friday-night crowd.

"Don't overdo the workouts or you'll hurt yourself," Luke said.

"I'm not in bad shape. I'm just toning a bit for the wedding," she told him, feeling suddenly shy as she faced him and ridiculously intimate with just the two of them alone in an asphalt parking lot. What could be more romantic?

A stray breeze lifted her hair and blew a few strands across her face. He lifted them off her cheek and tucked them behind her ear, making the gesture both friendly and more. "I'd like to see you again," he said, and stepped closer.

"You would?" She felt breathless. Option One was about half a step away and she found herself anticipating the feel of his mouth on hers.

"Will you?"

Maybe he needed a book for the really heavy stuff, but at light flirtation and conversation, Luke was terrific. She did want to spend more time with him. She felt the pull between them and wondered how his kisses were, prepared to be generous in her evaluation. "Yes," she said, and her lips parted and her eyes drifted to half-mast.

"Good." He sounded matter-of-fact. "I'll call you."

"Call me." She heard her own words soft and sleepy and seeming to come from far away. What had happened to the kiss that hovered between them like the smell of rain just before it pours?

Then it hit her that he'd been asking her about going out again. He must be reciting lines from the book, since they had a standing Friday night date. And she'd been mistaken. Imagining he meant... Damn, that book must be good.

"Where's your car?"

Refusing to act like a stuttering fool for one more second, she pulled her thoughts together, snapped her eyelids open and her lips shut. "This way."

He waited at her side while she unlocked her car door, then he surprised her by opening it for her. As she went to slide in, he stopped her with a hand on her shoulder, so she turned to him.

"I'll call you," he said again, then kissed her cheek.

The gesture didn't suit him somehow, and seemed almost deliberate. "Is that in the book?" she asked tartly.

"Yep."

She nodded, thinking it was going to be a long and tedious four weeks, then turned to slide behind the wheel, wondering if she'd stop on the way home for a video so her Friday evening wasn't a complete waste.

Before she'd finished the thought, she felt him

whirl her body 'round and slap his lips on hers, hot and demanding. Her pulse jumped and her heart started to race. His mouth soothed and demanded, offered and possessed, so she felt dizzy with conflicting sensations. She sighed softly and leaned into him. As she'd guessed, he tasted like cold beer, but there were hints of hot male there, too. Instinctively she responded, until he pulled away, leaving her aroused and unsatisfied.

"Was that—" she began breathlessly.

"My own interpretation."

She smiled. He was obviously a quick study. "Better."

5

"YOU'RE JUST LIKE YOUR father."

The familiar mix of emotions jumbled in Luke's belly at those oft-heard words. Pride first, then the guilt. Because when his mother repeated that line she'd been tossing at him since he was a kid, she didn't mean it as a compliment.

In all the years she'd thrown his likeness to his father in his face, he'd never come up with a response that would both satisfy his mother and prevent her from ever repeating the words.

"Pass the jam," was the best he could come up with at this Saturday-morning brunch at his mom's. The family tried to get together every week or two and, since Stacy, the second youngest, had started working Sunday nights at the telephone company, they'd changed the customary Sunday night dinner to a weekend brunch. It was usually on Saturdays so his mom could attend church on Sunday.

Roberta Lawson was still a beautiful woman, though she didn't bother much with her appearance anymore. "What's the point?" she'd say when one of the kids would put a makeup kit in her Christmas stocking or her daughters would suggest a girls' day out shopping. "Nobody wants to look at me. And if you're smart, you won't want them looking at you, either. You know what looking leads to and that's nothing but trouble.''

"How can you be such a Jewish mother when we're not even Jewish?" Deandra complained. The eldest of his three sisters, she was the one Luke was closest to, and the one most likely to jump to his defense when he, the only male in the family, came under attack for all men. Or his father.

His sisters were all gorgeous, but Deandra was cover-model stunning. All black, wavy hair, milk-white skin, big green eyes and bee-stung lips. She was also a brilliant scientist, which always gave him a kick when he'd watch yet another guy trip on his tongue as she walked by, totally oblivious to the havoc she caused.

"Ha, Jewish mothers. How many Jewish mothers do you know whose husbands are getting married for the fifth time?"

Luke caught Deandra's eye and she grimaced. They'd tried to keep their dad's most recent nuptials from their mom; obviously they hadn't succeeded.

"How did you find out?" Luke asked.

"Not from any of you." His mother sent a condemning glare around the table, skewering each of them as it passed.

"Mom, we didn't want you to be hurt," Stacy mumbled. A younger, not quite so stunning version of Deandra, Stacy was the only one still living at home and remained closest to their mother.

"It doesn't hurt anymore. I just feel sorry for him. I really do. I bet she's younger than you, Deandra. She'll want children. Mark my words. What does a fifty-three-year-old man want with babies? He should spend some time with the children he's already got.''

Since three of Henry Lawson's marriages had produced kids, there were half brothers and sisters all over the place. They got together every summer at their dad's cabin on Lummi Island, with the bunkhouse out back to contain all his offspring. Once again, Luke wondered how a basically decent man such as his father could screw up so badly again and again, leaving confused children scattered in his wake like so much flotsam and jetsam.

His mom shook her head sadly. ''Just wait till you get married.''

None of them was showing the slightest indication of doing so. Luke had a feeling none of them wanted to re-create the circumstances of their own childhoods. Not that their memories were bad—his mom always did her best—but they weren't all picnics and smiling family photos, either.

Deandra jumped to her feet and started clearing dishes. Luke was only too happy to pitch in. The faster they got the kitchen cleaned, the sooner they could split. He loved his mom, and he'd already changed the washers in her sinks and the oil in her car before sitting down to omelettes and toast. But listening to her rant only made his belly burn. He couldn't help her, and when she compared him to his father he was defenseless, because he knew she was right.

He *was* just like his old man. He loved women. And when he got bored with the one he was with, he knew there'd be another just around the corner.

Deandra and he made their escape together and he

walked her to her car then paused as she unlocked it and opened the door. But she didn't get in right away. She faced him with concern in her gorgeous eyes.

"She doesn't mean it, you know," his sister said, laying a hand on his wrist.

"Sure she does." He took Deandra's hand. "And she's right. But there's nothing I can do to change what Dad did to her—to all of us—any more than I can change my own genes."

She nodded and shook her hair back. "So, are you going to his latest wedding?"

"Haven't missed one yet. He asked me to be his best man."

Amusement flickered in her eyes. "The guy's got nerve. Are you going to?"

"Yeah. I guess. Are you going?"

"I always tell myself I won't, and then I go. I know he's an ass and he's hurt Mom, but…" She sighed and ran her index finger along the top of her car door. "He's our father and I don't think he meant to hurt anybody. It's as though he can't help himself."

Luke nodded. "You bringing a date?"

"I'll probably bring Sid." Sid was a senior scientist in the lab where she worked. A brilliant man, but no party animal.

Luke shuddered. "Every time I see Sid I get the feeling he's planning to clone me or something."

His sister laughed. "Spoken like a true egomaniac. How about you? Are you bringing your latest?"

"How do you know I have a latest?"

"You always have a latest."

"I am sort of seeing someone. I might ask her. I'll

see.'' He hadn't even thought of taking a date to his father's wedding until Deandra mentioned it, but all at once he imagined Shari there. She was warm and personable, and he might actually enjoy himself if there was a nice woman with him. In fact, he'd been thinking of her more than he should since they'd parted last night.

That kiss he'd planted on her had been both spontaneous and quick. He'd stayed within the guidelines of chapter one, but only just. If he'd lingered and toyed with her mouth, given her a taste of what he'd like to do with her...well, that would have been cheating. So he'd kept the lip contact agonizingly brief. But oh, how he'd wanted to take his time exploring, teasing, exciting.

He'd roared home and flipped through the book only to discover that nothing but frustration awaited him if he followed the book religiously, one chapter a week. He might not know all about the sex life of millipedes, which for some reason his sister was keen on, but he knew one thing—he couldn't wait a month to make love to Shari.

"Hello?" His sister's voice brought him back from the fantasy that had bloomed in his head, a scenario from chapter fourteen—advanced lovemaking techniques. "Where did you go?"

He blinked his eyes a few times. "Sorry. I think I've done a really stupid thing."

Seconds passed. "Well, I don't seem to have fainted from shock. Tell me about it."

So he did. Deandra was his sister, but also one of

his closest friends. And, apart from being as commitment-phobic as the rest of his sibs, she was smart about people. Well, she was smart about everything. He had a feeling it would take every neuron in her genius-size brain to find a way out of this one.

She hooted with laughter when he described the scene where his book fell out in front of Shari. And while she never laughed out loud again during his recital, he had a feeling she was calling on all her willpower. By the time he got to the part where he'd smacked a closemouthed kiss on Shari and promised to call, his sister sounded as though she had a bad head cold, sniffing and making coughlike sounds in the back of her throat.

"So what do you think?" he finished.

"You *are* a total moron. That's what I think."

"Come on. You're a scientist. I thought you'd understand how much I wanted to verify my hypothesis."

She patted his cheek with a cool palm. "You want to have sex with your test subject. Very scientific."

He groaned out loud. "And I don't want to wait four more weeks to do it."

"So call her."

"Huh?"

"In the parking lot, after you kissed her like she was your ailing grandmother, you said you'd call her. So call her. Do two chapters a week if you're so anxious to get your tongue in her mouth—"

"Deandra, has anyone ever told you you're brilliant?"

Her green eyes tilted like a cat's when she smiled. "Most everyone gets 'round to it eventually."

LUKE WHISTLED as he flipped through his how-to book. He was almost certain...ah, yes. Here it was, near the beginning of chapter two.

> The small gift, the token of regard, may be considered old-fashioned by some, and that's fine by us because it gives us an advantage. Remember this—the florist is your friend. Nothing melts a woman's heart like a box full of greenery. But do be creative...

He'd been smart enough to include a list of what messages different flowers imparted. He scanned the list and decided that sometimes in-your-face obvious was the way to go. A red rose. For passion.

Oh, yeah.

He found the number of his favorite local florist on his Rolodex and then stood with the phone in his hand. How many? It was never easy. A dozen was overeager. One seemed chintzy. So he settled on half a dozen.

The note for the card was easy. *Thinking of you,* it said. And she couldn't possibly know how true that was.

He put the coffeepot on and settled at the computer desk in his bedroom to write his monthly column for *Hey, Girl,* a woman's magazine in which he gave a guy's perspective on sex and dating. He'd been having trouble coming up with a theme, and suddenly, there it was. "What he's really trying to say when he sends you flowers."

He was editing the completed column when his

phone rang. He checked the call display and grinned. Shari.

"Thank you for the roses. They're beautiful. You didn't have to." She sounded a little flustered. Embarrassed even.

"They're a small thank-you for helping me out." And a step toward chapter five. But she didn't have to know that.

"You're welcome," she said primly.

"How's the fitness program?"

She groaned. "I'm killing myself. The weights, the treadmill. And don't get me started on the sit-ups."

He laughed. "The gym makes it seem too much like work. You should get outside for a bike ride or a hike."

"You're probably right. But there's a gym at school, plus the one in our building, so it's easy."

On an impulse, he checked tomorrow's weather on the Internet. The forecast was for sunshine, which had to be a sign. "Why don't I take you on my favorite hiking trail tomorrow? The weather's supposed to be good."

"Oh, um…I wasn't expecting…I don't know…I wasn't expecting to see you until Friday."

He rolled his eyes. Couldn't she cut him some slack? "I'm not inviting you as a date, but as your personal trainer. That's close to a medical professional."

She chuckled. "Since when are you a personal trainer?"

Since five seconds ago. "You should give me a try. No obligation. We'll even split the supplies. You pack the lunch, I'll bring the water."

Once more he was treated to a reluctant chuckle. "Don't strain yourself over the water." He waited, and could imagine her weighing pros and cons until, finally, she agreed. "All right. But this better be good for an inch off my hips."

An inch off her hips would be a crime against nature in his opinion, but he'd grown up with enough sisters to keep his mouth shut. "I'll be at your door at eight tomorrow morning."

"All right."

"Oh, and Shari? Pack lots of sandwiches. I have a big appetite."

Then he grabbed his book to check out what he was supposed to do in chapter two.

Luke had to admit, he'd painted himself into a tight corner. Ha! More like nailed himself inside a Chinese puzzle box, he decided as he made himself a chicken clubhouse sandwich.

When he'd talked Shari into following the first four chapters of his book, he'd sentenced them to a month without sex. At the time he hadn't had a clue how much he'd want her, the way a man would drool over forbidden fruit.

If he didn't speed up the process, he was going to toss the book aside and forget about his science experiment. And yet, half the reason he wanted her so badly was knowing he couldn't have her. Maybe his willpower would weaken and he'd seduce her his way on his time, but not yet. Half the fun of this experiment was knowing it wasn't Luke Lawson seducing Shari, but Lance Flagstaff.

And so far, he wasn't doing such a bad job. Tomorrow, when he finessed her through chapter two without her realizing it, would be critical.

Luckily for him, his sister was smart enough to

have thought of a way to fast-track his way into an affair with Shari. In fact, he was so pleased with her suggestion he pushed the redial button and got the same florist. He sent another half dozen roses to his sister.

He demolished his sandwich, crunched a couple of apples and headed out to get some air and maybe stock up on some food at the market.

At least that was one appetite he could satisfy.

The more pressing one would have to wait. But, like a starving man at a banquet, he wasn't sure how much longer he could resist becoming intimate with Shari.

6

SHARI'S FIRST THOUGHT on waking was that she'd better not break a nail hiking, since she was growing them for the wedding.

"You'd think it was your wedding," Therese had chided after hearing about the all-out body sculpting, nail growing, clothes shopping and date-prepping program on which Shari had embarked.

Therese could mock her all she wanted, but Shari was determined to show B.J., Randy and their mutual friends that she was doing absolutely fine, thank you very much.

A naturally early riser, she had the lunches packed, her apartment tidied and still had time for a hundred sit-ups...well, seventy-three. But, as she rose, groaning, she vowed to get up to a hundred before the week was out.

She took the time to change the water for the roses that graced her coffee table, stopping to touch a silky red petal and then dip her head to catch its delicate scent.

Luke had sent her flowers. It was such a sweet gesture she smiled, almost immediately realizing he must have got the idea from that book, which had her shaking her head as she padded to the bathroom to add another layer of strengthening topcoat to her finger nails.

When he knocked on her door she was all ready. Then she saw him, and her pulse fluttered. She hadn't seen him since he'd kissed her in the parking lot the night before last. The contact of their lips had been so brief and yet hinted at so much, he'd left her feeling confused and somehow empty. Her tongue traced her lips without any planning on her part, and Luke's eyes darkened as he watched the gesture.

When she realized what she was doing she yanked her tongue back in her mouth. "Shall we go?"

She grabbed her packsack and they made their way to the parking garage where he led her to one of those macho SUVs that was so dusty and scratched she suspected he, unlike most SUV owners, actually took his off-road.

"The trail I'm thinking of takes around five hours round trip. That okay with you?"

If she'd known she'd be hiking for five hours she might have skipped the sit-ups. She flexed her leg muscles and confirmed they were still a little sore from yesterday's workout. Still, she only had three weeks left until the wedding. She imagined she'd have sore muscles most days. "Yes, fine."

"I like this trail. It follows a river and you get some nice views when you get up high."

They chatted on the drive there as though they were nothing but friends, but there was a silent pull, like the undertow of a seemingly placid sea, that hinted at more than friendship. She wondered if she'd been wise to let Luke talk her into this.

Once they set off on the hike she was suddenly

glad she'd come. The air smelled fresh and clean, of pine and new spring growth. Weedy wildflowers poked through the greenery. The sky above them was blue with a couple of cotton-candy clouds. Her muscles were warming and stretching as they walked, and she had to admit that five hours of this ought to be a major fat burner, thigh toner and butt firmer.

Birds, flowers, fresh green things, and the view... Well, mostly the view was of Luke striding ahead of her in shorts, which, as views went, was nice.

Although, as the trail steepened, the view began to seem less nice. In fact, the sight of those muscular legs striding ahead with perfect ease began to irritate her.

As he'd promised, he'd brought the water. He wore a belt with a pocket on each hip containing a water bottle.

"Hey," she said. Wheezed actually.

He didn't seem to have heard her. She glared at the jaunty gunslinger belt containing water bottles instead of six-shooters. "Hey!" she yelled.

"What's up?" He turned, and she could see that he wasn't even panting. Or sweating.

She, on the other hand, was pumping out perspiration like a garden sprinkler, and her ribs felt as though they were flapping like bird's wings as her lungs dragged in air.

"Need water."

He dug out a bottle and presented it to her. "I'll slow down. Sorry."

She glugged water thankfully. "No. It's fine." She'd be so thin and toned by the wedding, B.J. would barely recognize her. Ha.

"Drink as much as you like. I've got lots more in my pack."

After a couple of life-restoring breaths, she motioned Luke ahead, sneakily hanging on to the water bottle. She was certain she'd need it again soon.

After a while she noticed the ground had leveled, and from somewhere her body had tapped into a new burst of energy. "How are you doing?" Luke said, turning to her.

"I got my second wind," she replied, liking the way his T-shirt looked when he turned from the waist and it plastered against his chest. He must have perspired, after all, for it clung damply against his muscles. Yum. She felt her own chest tighten at the sight and involuntarily imagined how his chest would feel, naked, rubbing against hers. She had a feeling it would feel fantastic. There was nothing complex about that move. She could teach him how to ace it in no time.

Already she was thinking like a teacher. She couldn't help herself. She'd learned early to give her students small challenges to rev up their confidence for the tougher stuff.

A fine chest like that, rubbed against a woman's sensitive breasts, would get him enough oohs and aahs to give him some much-needed confidence. Of that she was certain.

Was she willing to go that extra step for him? She'd agreed to kissing, no more. Bare-chested rubbing was definitely an extra, thrown in out of the goodness of her heart.

However, he was being nice enough to act as her

personal trainer today, giving her an outdoor workout, so maybe she could afford to be generous.

She snuck another glance at his chest and wondered if it was hairy. She loved hairy chests. Yes, she thought as warmth gathered in her lower body, she was feeling generous.

In fact, maybe she was looking at this all wrong. Instead of letting Luke set the pace, she, with her experience and confidence, should take charge. For goodness' sake, she was the teacher, wasn't she? What was she doing letting the special ed kid stand at the front of the class and give the lecture? No wonder she'd felt frustrated. It was time to start doing what she did best. Teach.

As Luke resumed his murderous pace, she decided to think about something else. She couldn't afford to waste any energy on warming her erogenous zones. Right now she needed to keep her legs walking and her lungs inflating. Sexual impulses were the equivalent of a leaky fuel tank.

After another half an hour, she cracked and dug into her pack for the mountain mix she'd run out and bought, glad now she'd purchased the kind that included M&M's. She was certain the raisins and nuts and pumpkin seeds were going to do wonders for her energy and stamina, but, frankly, she needed the chocolate.

"How far do you think we've come?" she asked Luke. He stopped and turned, taking out his own water bottle and drinking deeply.

"I guess around three or four miles. Why?" He dug into the bag of trail mix she offered.

"I want to make sure I've earned another handful

of this stuff.'' She glanced into the bag. M&M's winked at her like precious jewels in a pirate's treasure chest. ''Who am I kidding? This is a case of desperate need.''

Luke chuckled. ''Come on. It's only another couple of miles to a nice picnic spot.''

A couple of miles. She could do that. She'd play a game with herself. For every fifteen minutes of hiking, she'd allow herself one chocolate treat.

Three candies later, Luke led her off the main trail and down a narrow path until they hit a grassy clearing overlooking the river. From their perch they could see a wide gravel shoal where the river formed a natural bay, and some logs and a larger meadow. An older couple was packing up a picnic. ''That's where the main trail leads,'' Luke said, ''but I like this spot better. It's more private.''

She glanced at him sharply, trying to gauge his meaning. Forgetting her own earlier thoughts about bare-chest rubbing, she narrowed her eyes in his direction. Did he have something private planned for her? If so, she'd be showing him right quick that only Friday was Total Moron day. Every other day of the week she expected him to act like a normal person.

However, as they unpacked the picnic she'd made and sat out under the sunshine, he didn't act remotely like a lover. Quite the opposite. He was so casual she relaxed completely.

She sighed with relief as she eased down onto the sun-warmed grass.

''Tired?'' he asked, stretching out.

''It's been a while since I hiked,'' she admitted. Her feet felt hot and stifled in the heavy boots. Oh, what the hell. Swiftly she undid her hiking boots, yanked them off and then slipped off the scratchy wool socks.

Mmm. A light breeze blew gently against her hot toes and she wiggled them, enjoying the almost sexual feeling of warm sun, soft grass and free-flowing air on her toes. She glanced up to see Luke staring at her feet, fierce concentration on his face. Something about his expression sent a shaft of heat stabbing her belly.

He shifted his gaze to her face and they stared at each other for a single, earth-stopping moment.

She swallowed and broke the spell by reaching for her packsack and digging out the lunch. "I hope you like ham and cheese. I wasn't sure."

"Sounds great," he said, sounding much less flustered than she.

Careful not to let any of her skin touch any of his, she passed him a double-decker sandwich.

He unwrapped it and took a bite. "It's good. Thanks."

She bit into her own single sandwich and settled back against a granite boulder.

By the time they got through her homemade, oat-meal-chocolate-chip cookies to the plums, she'd relaxed completely. The odd moment of sexual awareness between her and Luke might never have happened. He was acting like a casual hiking companion—an acquaintance, nothing more.

No sooner did she realize that than she wondered why he wasn't taking the opportunity to further their lessons now that he had her in a secluded outdoor setting complete with dappled sunlight, a light spring breeze, soft, cushiony, fragrant green grass and privacy. This place was a postcard for intimate romantic trysts.

Perhaps he was too shy, or felt it was inappropriate outside of their agreed Fridays.

Much as she appreciated his discretion, she was a big believer in teaching moments—those opportunities that occur naturally when a lesson sticks because the student is in the right frame of mind to learn.

This felt very much like one of those moments. Besides, she'd been thinking about his chest for several miles now. She shot him a glance from under her lashes. He was packing his plum pits in the plastic wrap from his sandwich, which looked like getting-ready-to-hike-some-more movements to her. She was nowhere near ready for more hiking.

Everything seemed to point to taking advantage of this perfect teaching moment, especially when she noticed a drop of plum juice on his chin.

She scooted closer to Luke until he glanced up at her, brows slightly raised.

"You missed some plum," she said softly. Keeping her gaze on his she caught the gleaming purple drop with her thumb and rubbed it gently against his bottom lip. "I love plums," she said, and lowered her mouth oh, so slowly to his. She hovered, her lips almost touching, then let her tongue sweep across his full lower lip from corner to corner.

Mmm. She breathed, tasting plum and warm male, before fitting her mouth to his.

Oh, he was warm and he tasted wonderful. He was also restrained. A lot of guys would have flipped her onto her back by now and would have wrested control of the kiss, but Luke didn't do that. Whether because of uncertainty or shyness, he was leaving her in charge.

Seemed a shame to waste such a great opportunity for furthering Luke's education.

She found she enjoyed taking the lead, which gave her a heady sense of power. She gazed into his eyes and saw a churning blend of passion and excitement. She couldn't resist the urge to go back to his mouth for more.

While he might be slow to take over the lead, he managed to keep up with her just fine. When she withdrew her tongue from his mouth, his followed, dipping in and teasing her mouth in the identical way she'd teased his. It was an incredible turn-on, a very adult form of follow the leader.

While heat began to build in her body, she kept recalling the sight of his damp T-shirt outlining his muscular chest. She wanted to see it. Needed to see it. Had to see it.

With a quick glance to confirm they still had complete privacy, she slipped a hand under the hem of his shirt and pulled.

He rose slightly, curling his spine to help her and what that curl did to his abdomen made her weaker at the knees than she already was. Muscle, hard and ropy, striped his belly. As the shirt rose it revealed a nicely contoured chest with just the right amount of reddish-brown hair.

"Nice," she sighed, her enthusiasm overcoming her sense as she trailed her fingertips across the tawny skin of his chest and burrowed into the springy hair. "You have the perfect amount of chest hair."

"How do you measure perfect?" His voice was joking, but he sounded a little embarrassed at the way she was gushing over him. He must be kind of shy. Probably that's where his problem originated, because there was nothing wrong with him that she could tell. He was gorgeous, smelled good, tasted good and the evidence of his arousal nudged against her when she surprised them both by rolling on top of him.

"I guess it's personal taste. Smooth as a baby's bum is too little for me. But shag rug is too much."

Just running her fingers over him wasn't going to be enough. Her own chest ached to join the party.

Another teaching moment was in front of them. She gazed down at him. "I'm feeling pretty aroused," she murmured, and had the pleasure of watching his eyes darken. Just telling him her feelings was making her squirm.

He swallowed audibly.

Arching her spine, like a cat stretching, she said, "Can you tell?"

His gaze dropped to her chest where the tight, tingling sensation confirmed that her nipples were doing their best to call attention to themselves. *Good boy. Go to the head of the class.*

He nodded.

"How can you tell?"

He raised his gaze—was that a wicked glint of humor? It was gone so fast she must have imagined it. He lifted a hand to her face—no, no, no, that's not where she wanted to feel his hand!—and traced her cheek. "You're flushed."

She was?

He ran a finger over her mouth, so shocking and

unexpected that she quivered. "Your lips are swollen."

She licked her lips and nodded.

"Heart rate's elevated," he continued. Good. The heart was in the chest. His observations were moving him in the right direction. Why didn't he touch her tingling breasts?

"Breathing's a little fast." The man was checking her out like a racehorse gearing up for the Kentucky Derby. Still, he was very observant.

"That's great," she said. "You only missed one symptom. Well, two actually." Tired of waiting for him to pick up on her body's obvious hints, she took his hands and placed his palms on her breasts where her tightened nipples strained.

He cupped them lightly and she almost moaned. She didn't remember the last time she'd felt so…so sexy. But all he did was move his palms around, and she wanted so much more. He was obviously waiting for her to make the next move, but she wanted to give him the confidence to make one of his own.

"Unbutton my top," she suggested softly, glad she'd worn a sleeveless cotton shirt rather than a T-shirt.

His gaze rose to hers and his eyes seemed to burn, then he did as she asked, starting at her throat and working his way down slowly. He was probably nervous and feeling hesitant, which must be why he was taking his damned time when she wanted him to rip the shirt off and pull her down against him.

"You should wear a sports bra," he said when he spread the two sides of her shirt. "Better support."

"I like this one. Easier access." Deciding it was

time for teacher to take control once more of the lesson, she reached for the front clasp and snapped her bra open, pulling the cups apart slowly, revealing herself to him.

Luke stared at her breasts as though he'd never seen such things before. After a long, silent moment, when she felt his gaze on her with such intensity she expected scorch marks, he said, "Thank you."

She tipped her head back and let the sun touch her face, knowing the posture made her look like the figurehead on the prow of a ship. That's a little how she felt, too. Sailing into uncharted waters, nipples first. A light breeze tousled her hair and teased her naked chest. "Do you want to touch them?"

"You have no idea." His voice was as soft as the breeze. She felt him shift and then his hands were warm where the air had been cool. Taking her weight on her knees, she freed her arms so she could cup her hands over his and show him how she liked to be touched.

She felt his fingers beneath hers as together they plumped and rubbed her breasts just the way she liked. Then, linking her fingers with his, she lowered her head so she was kissing him again, deeper this time. As her chest came into contact with his, a low hum began vibrating in the back of her throat. He was so warm and furry and muscular. She wrapped her arms around him and lay flush against his body, feeling wonderful.

Far, far below them she heard a dog bark. If she scooted to the edge of the bluff she could look down and see the animal's owners. For all she knew there were a hundred people down there, but up here it was private and secluded.

Her bare legs tangled with his, her toes stubbing against his big leather boots. Deciding to use the unyielding leather to her advantage, she braced her feet against them and pushed herself up and down, gasping at the sensations as her sensitive breasts scraped against hair and muscle and warm, warm skin.

Oh, boy. This was just too much like mimicking sex. She felt the way her body was preparing to be entered, everything tingling and softening—rather eagerly, too. It was warm enough, private enough, and they were both excited enough. She imagined him, lunging like a puppy, eager and grateful, and she felt a deep stirring to give him a lesson that would blow his mind. But, even as the idea took hold, warning bells started clamoring in her head. She wasn't prepared to go any further. She hadn't intended to include sex play with the picnic and she certainly hadn't packed condoms along with the trail mix.

Abruptly, she stopped moving, trying to find a graceful exit line. Even though she was trying to remain still, her chest was heaving as though she'd just run straight up this hill. Of course, Luke's chest was doing the same; so even without any effort from her, there was plenty of chest rubbing going on. And it felt so damn good.

Luke smiled up at her and tucked a stray curl behind her ear. "We should probably get going. What kind of personal trainer lets you take a two-hour lunch break?"

Swallowing her astonishment that he was calling a

halt, she forced a casual smile to her own face. ''Right.''

She pulled her clothing back together and put her hiking boots on. He stuffed himself into his shirt, and they gathered up their things.

She couldn't believe he'd called time-out. She'd planned to do that. What kind of man, in a clinch with a half-naked woman, didn't do his level best to get the other half naked?

LUKE FELT LIKE A PRIZE ass. The way he was acting, Shari was going to think he was gay.

What man in the world wouldn't get on his bended knee and beg Shari Wilson for everything she was willing to give? Even just one single taste of her glorious breasts and he could have died happy.

But if he'd had so much as a lick, so much as one firm, berry-ripe nipple rubbing against his tongue, he would have been lost and begging. Ruining his chance to prove his book worked.

And so far, in spite of the fact he was suffering more pent-up sexual frustration than a teenager, he had to admit the book was working amazingly well. Shari had pretty much taken care of chapter two today all on her own.

One glance at her stunned and frustrated countenance had him stifling a grin. If she had any idea how many frustrated urges he was also trying to stifle right now she'd be feeling pretty damn full of herself. The lady was amazing, so generous and sexy and…sweet.

She did her best to impart technique to him without appearing to teach, leaving his ego intact, although she was pretty much shredding his self-control.

Had he ever wanted a woman this much? He tried to recall, but he didn't think so.

Probably that was simply because of his self-imposed restrictions. He was playing this one by the book. By his book. And he'd never wanted so badly to break all the rules.

Shari took the lead for the return trip, going so fast she verged on a trot. He couldn't blame her. If she was feeling half as charged as he was, she had a lot of free-floating sexual energy to burn.

He let her go ahead because he understood that she needed the outlet, but it wasn't easy walking behind her and watching the sway of her hips, the way the sun stroked her long, sexy legs—rendered even more feminine by the clunky hikers and gray wool socks.

Still, it was better focusing on her back view than letting himself drift into reverie about the sight of her half-naked front and the feel of her body snugged against his.

And he especially didn't want to wonder about what would have happened if he'd followed his urge to flip her onto her back and put his mouth to her breasts, trailed his tongue down her smooth belly, unfastened her shorts and... Nope, he wasn't going there. Not today.

By the time they got back to the car he was amazed at himself. He'd had a warm and willing woman in his arms and he'd stopped himself indulging in all of her sweetness because of a stupid book? For the second time in as many weeks he felt like whacking himself over the head with the stupid thing.

Ahead of him, Shari pulled out the trail mix and he watched her pick out every one of the colored chocolate candies and pop them into her mouth. Red, yellow, blue, brown, she ate them one at a time, pushing them beneath her lips, which were still plump and juicy from kissing him.

His hands literally twitched to take her in his arms and find a handy spot somewhere in the bushes where they could enjoy each other uninterrupted.

Sex for TMs was only a book. Paper and ink. Shari was flesh and blood. He couldn't stop thinking about how she'd looked with the sun on her breasts, the dusky-tipped nipples taunting him. He had to see them again, touch them again, taste them…the hell with the book.

Shari routed through the trail mix and then on a muffled curse, which he assumed meant she'd already gobbled the last of the M&M's, shoved the bag into her pocket.

"Shari," he called to her.

She didn't even turn around. "Hurry up. I have to get to a store." She sounded like a heavy smoker having a serious nicotine fit. "I need more M&M's."

7
_____

SHARI PACED HER APARTMENT feeling as jumpy as a claustrophobic tiger in a cage.

This was ridiculous! It was just sex.

Well, no. It wasn't just sex. In fact it wasn't sex at all and that was the source of her frustration. She wanted Luke. Mr. Clueless who halted the action more often than a shy virgin.

She gasped and paused midpace. Was he…?

No. He must be thirty. Impossible he'd never had sex.

And yet, while he was clearly turned on by her, he was so clueless, ambivalent or uninterested that he wasn't taking any initiative at all. No wonder the man needed a how-to book.

Ever since their hike yesterday she'd felt buzzy and strange, almost jumping out of her own skin with lust. It was crazy. Normally she left it to the men in her life to tamp down lust while her relationships took a predictable path. They wanted in her pants and, when she decided she liked them enough and the time was right, she let them.

Never in all her life had she wanted in a man's pants and he was keeping them zipped.

She paced again. Wondering if the ache in her womb was chronic. If there was a pill she could take to relieve it she would, but she knew damn well there was only one cure for her ailments. Hot, sweaty sex. The sooner the better.

Chapters schmapters, she wasn't waiting until Friday. Luke wanted some lessons in how to please a woman? He was about to get the most important lesson of them all.

She was a fine teacher if she did say so herself. And he'd proven himself a fairly apt student. It was time to do what was often done with talented, advanced learners. He was about to be accelerated.

She had to plan this carefully, though. Men were visual creatures. She needed to send him an unmistakable message that she wanted him in the most intimate way a woman could want a man.

She stopped pacing as a tiger's smile curled her lips.

Stomping into the bathroom she turned on the faucets to pour herself a bath, taking her favorite scented bath salts off the shelf. She threw in a healthy handful and from her medicine cabinet pulled out ylang-ylang essential oil—a scent to inspire the libido.

Luke was going to get a lesson he'd never forget.

LUKE HADN'T BELIEVED he'd end up glad of the Hikus Interruptus interlude, but somehow the frustration had been rechanneled into creativity. He'd come home last night and, after Shari had issued a curt goodbye, stood wrestling with himself until sweat broke out on his brow. Twice he started for his door, intending to run upstairs and damn well pound on Shari's door until she opened it, the hell with the book.

Had he ever in his life turned away from a woman with Do Me Baby in her eyes, her body primed and ready for him?

He groaned. Of course, he hadn't. Only a man numb from the waist down could do that.

And he was far from that. He could still feel her body pressed against him, her head thrown back to enjoy the sun. She'd looked magnificent.

He shook his head like a horse shaking off flies. If he spent the night in, he'd be knocking on Shari's door within the hour. He'd made it this far, he'd reread chapters three and four and would try to fit them in this week. By Friday—maybe sooner if she decided to cut him some slack—he'd be getting into the serious stuff and by chapter six he'd be easing into heaven.

After a quick shower, he changed into black jeans and a loud come-and-get-me Hawaiian-print shirt, and walked the few blocks to his favorite watering hole.

The smell of beer mingled with the scents of the justly famous burgers. Laszlo's was crowded with people having a good time. Bypassing the wooden booths, he headed for the U-shaped bar, already noting the number of women here. He nodded to a couple of people he knew, found a stool and ordered a beer. The bartender was a middle-aged Slavic guy and, since Luke was a lot more interested in women who were nowhere near middle age, he turned so he was facing the crowd. One of the reasons Laszlo's worked was that patrons tended to stand around and mingle.

He'd socialize in a minute. For now he'd simply sit back and watch the action, the seduction game he'd played so often and written about in countless magazine articles. The beer was ice-cold and crackled on his tongue. Laszlo's was hopping. He scanned the place for a woman to saunter over to and start up a conversation.

Near the door, a shapely female back caught his attention. Rich chestnut curls spilled down her long, slim back. She was tall, and exuded confidence even from this view. His shoulders jerked forward and his babe radar went on full-alert. That looked like...but even as the thought formed, the woman turned to say something to the guy standing beside her and he registered that it wasn't Shari. And he knew in that moment that no one else would do for him tonight.

He ordered a burger, finished the beer, made some desultory conversation with a fellow beside him and left.

He'd planned to render himself numb all over, but he didn't feel like dealing with crowds and noise, and besides, if he stayed he was liable to go home with the first willing woman, which wouldn't help at all.

He only wanted one woman. The one he'd already rejected today.

As he entered his apartment the frustrated sexual energy still fizzed within him and he knew he wouldn't sleep. He flipped on the TV, but nothing held his attention. He dropped to the carpet and did fifty push-ups, then groaned when he realized he was thinking about Shari and her daily sit-ups and push-ups and how much he wished she were under him right now.

It was too early to go to bed, and the only place he really wanted to be—one floor up and one apartment over—he had a strong feeling he wasn't welcome.

Desperate for distraction, he flicked on his computer and pulled up the file of his novel. He hadn't worked on it in a while with the how-to book consuming him, but maybe tonight it would keep him focused on something other than his physical desire.

He settled into his chair and decided to play with the book for a few hours. It was a psychological thriller, his play project when he was between magazine and newspaper assignments. One day, he might try fiction seriously, but it was easier work and easy money to stay with what he knew.

Reading over the first four chapters, which were all he had written, he got pulled into the series of gruesome murders and the burned-out cop who was close to a breakdown. Luke remembered now why he'd stopped writing after chapter four. He'd put the poor sucker in a psych ward and didn't know how he was going to get him out...

No wonder he'd been drawn to open this particular computer file. The irony wasn't lost on him. Luke was as helplessly locked in torment as his hero.

He sat there, tapping keys without typing anything, imagining the hero's dilemma. He was a cop who'd spent his whole career—his entire life—abiding by and enforcing the rules. Now he had to break the rules. He had to escape from the prison his preconceived notions had locked him into.

He had to break out.

Of course! Suddenly Luke's fingers were flying over the keyboard. He couldn't type fast enough to keep up with his thoughts.

At some point he became aware that his neck ached. He glanced at the clock. It was four in the morning. He could go to bed, but he wasn't a bit tired and the killer was about to strike again. Oh, well. It wasn't as though Luke had to be anywhere tomorrow. One of the joys of his work was setting his own schedule. He stood, stretched and made his way to the kitchen to brew a pot of coffee.

Then he went back to work.

Hours later, the coffeepot was empty. He brewed another.

Time simply ceased to matter. His phone rang a couple of times, but he ignored it. Not only did his hero burn for justice, but he also burned physically for the woman—the psychiatrist on his case—who could both save and damn him.

Luke glanced up at last, feeling his eyes ache. His muscles were stiff from the combined torture of sitting in one position too long, struggling through the tension of solving murders and coming to terms with his main character's mental health. But Luke had in front of him several solid new chapters and a rough road map for the rest of the book.

He leaned back in his chair, rubbing his closed eyes with his palms, tired but satisfied. Not as satisfied as he'd feel after a night of hot sex with Shari Wilson perhaps, but satisfied in a bone-deep sense.

He stared at the gray words darkening his screen and a quiver of excitement raced through him. What if this wasn't simply for fun? What if he was writing an honest-to-God marketable thriller?

The possibility had him running his fingers across his stubbled chin. What if?

He struggled to his feet with an unreal sense of timelessness. He hadn't pulled an all-nighter like that since college. He checked the clock. Seven. For one bizarre second he thought it was seven in the morning, then he realized it was seven at night. He'd worked just over twenty-four hours. Fueled by nothing but coffee and some serious sexual frustration.

He grinned stupidly. A few more weeks of trying to stay away from the woman upstairs and he'd have an entire series of murder mysteries.

His stomach did a queasy roll from all the coffee and lack of food. Usually, Luke ate constantly, but he'd been too absorbed to care about eating. Now he needed a decent meal, a shower and sleep, but the vestiges of manic energy still crackled around him and some of the scenes he'd written lingered like dream images. After all those hours cooped up, he needed to move.

Changing into running gear, he headed out to the street feeling like a long-distance traveler just emerging from an aircraft into an exotic setting. His body might be in Seattle but his mind was still in the book, he discovered, as he found his rhythm and followed the ribbon of pavement in the dusk. At some point it had rained, for the streets were slick with wet, and dark clouds hovered, letting him know that more rain was on its way. He'd lived in the Pacific Northwest long enough to pretty much ignore the rain.

As he splashed through a puddle, he realized he needed to let the villain figure out what Luke, the author, already knew. That his cop hero relied on routines to function. Throw him off stride and he was dramatically weakened.

How to give this information to the villain in a way the reader would buy? Suddenly it was important to Luke what the reader thought because some time in the night this novel had moved from being his little hobby to the next phase in his career.

There was a woman in the book, naturally. The psychiatrist helping the cop. Where before she'd lacked substance as a character, she'd come, during the night, to combine Deandra's fierce focus, Shari's looks and his mother's stubbornness. There was more of Shari in his fictitious doc than looks. He'd tried to imbue his character with that innate respect for people's feelings, and the desire to help them that Shari had displayed in their "lessons."

When he passed the Danish bakery that was his three-mile marker, he realized he'd gone farther than he intended.

The bakery was closed, nothing in the window but day-old bread already packaged to sell off tomorrow and the fancy cakes in the refrigerated display case. Even so, the sight was enough to make his stomach curl on itself unpleasantly.

He turned toward home wishing he hadn't jogged so far. He was literally running on coffee and adrenaline and both tanks were close to empty.

He'd never been so pleased to see his apartment building. Trembling with fatigue and hunger, he dragged himself in the door, hauled himself into the shower, shaved and decided he'd take himself out for a good dinner before hitting the sack.

In the steamy bathroom mirror his eyes were blood-shot, but he didn't care. The lost sleep and skipped meals had been worth the sacrifice. He'd never felt as excited about anything he'd written.

The phone rang while he was heading for the door debating steak versus pasta. He checked his call display, intending to ignore the call, only to grab the receiver when he saw it was S. Wilson calling.

Shari.

"Hello?" His voice sounded rusty and he realized he hadn't spoken in more than twenty-four hours.

"Luke, it's Shari." She sounded odd and, after spending all night with a twisted, sadistic murderer, Luke's system began to jump.

"Is everything okay?"

"I need you to come up here. Now," was all she said before cutting the connection.

"Shari?" he yelled into the phone before throwing it on the table and heading out the door at a run.

He tore up the stairs faster than he'd ever run in his life, reaching her door in less than a minute from the time she'd called. "Shari?"

He pounded on the door and it opened slightly. His panicked brain realized there was a shoe stuck in the door holding it ajar.

He shoved through, wishing he had something other than his bare hands to use as a weapon. Somehow, in his fatigued brain, he'd known the killer would go after the psychiatrist as the surest way to destroy the cop. Luke had to stop him.

It took a second or two for panic to recede and amazement to take its place.

Shari Wilson stood in the middle of her apartment living room. There were candles scattered around the place sending dancing flames and some kind of exotic scent into the air.

Soft music played, but all of that registered only in the haziest fashion.

For Shari was spectacularly, gloriously, naked.

8

THERE WASN'T ENOUGH fuel in Luke's body to power both his brain and his groin. Since he was a man with his priorities straight, all the blood rushed to his cock as he stared at her candlelit flesh, which looked pink and gold in the dancing light.

Sadly, the rush of blood to his groin caused immediate energy-rationing elsewhere. Even as he took a step toward her luscious, naked body, spots danced in front of his eyes, then started connecting until his vision faded like a computer screen once the off button was pushed.

"Luke," Shari called as his face paled and he staggered. "Luke!"

His eyes rolled up and he dropped to the ground like felled timber.

Luke woke with nausea in his belly and a blinding pain in his head. It took a few moments for his vision to clear, so he simply lay very still on Shari's floor.

"Are you okay?" she asked, dropping to her knees beside him. His eyeballs hurt, but he moved them, anyway, only to discover she'd donned a bathrobe while he was unconscious.

He didn't know which of them was the more embarrassed. "I'd be just as happy if I'd fallen right through the floor into my next-door neighbor's suite."

She smiled and her blush receded a little. "It was my fault. I guess I gave you a shock." She pulled the belt of the robe tighter.

He couldn't lie there on the floor any longer staring up at her. Hoping he wouldn't humiliate himself again, he struggled to his elbow and sat up. "Whew. Sorry. No sleep last night. I haven't eaten all day. Only coffee and then I went running and…well, sorry."

She'd called him for a reason, and even as muddled and thick as his head felt, he didn't have to be a genius to realize the lady had had seduction in mind. A quick glance showed that was now off the agenda. Goodbye forever had most likely replaced it.

Still, she looked sympathetic, and vaguely guilty as though she'd behaved inappropriately. "Of the men who've seen me naked, you're the first one who ever fainted. Do you faint often?"

"Faint? I didn't faint! I…passed out. First time. I'm going to crawl back to my apartment now, eat, then think about throwing myself out the window."

"You're only on the second floor."

"Good thing. I could kill myself if it was higher. I'm going for the grand gesture here, not the after-life."

She smiled, and seemed to struggle with herself. "You really look pale. I've got some pasta I could feed you. Would that help?"

Gratitude filled him. She wasn't going to throw him out on his sorry ass. He'd embarrassed her, made a fool of himself, and she was going to feed him.

He rose shakily to his feet. "You are a rare and

wonderful woman,'' he said, lifting her left hand and
kissing the knuckles.

Shari had no idea what had possessed her to offer
the man on her floor dinner. Maybe it was the mortified expression on his face as he stared up at her,
and some feeling of guilt for staging a blatant seduction act before he'd graduated from chapter two of
the sex manual. Talk about information overload. No
wonder the poor man had thrown a breaker.

If it weren't so damned humiliating, it would be
sort of funny. Well, if it happened to someone else,
it would be pretty funny.

Knowing she couldn't possibly spend any more
time in her bathrobe when both of them must be
keenly aware she had nothing on beneath it, she put
the lasagna she'd assembled earlier in the oven and
then, with a barely coherent excuse, dashed to her
bedroom to dress. She hoped Luke would never suspect that she'd intended him to eat lasagna all along,
only when she'd prepared it, she'd imagined them
eating it after making love, not after she'd scraped
him off her broadloom.

She threw on jeans and a loose cotton sweater and
emerged only to realize her apartment was still lit by
candlelight. Trying to act casual, she flipped on lights,
noticing that Luke still didn't look all that hot.

''You're not sick, are you?'' She contemplated
placing her hand on his forehead to check for fever,
but the way their evening was going that might throw
him into anaphylactic shock.

''No.'' He rolled his shoulders. ''I'm just tired. I
told you I didn't sleep last night.''

''Right.'' She strode into the kitchen, hoping at

least that what she was doing was striding and not flouncing. "You mentioned that already."

And just what—or who—had kept poor Luke up all night when he'd summarily rejected her advances halfway up a mountainside? Instead of feeding him lasagna she should probably be dumping it on his head.

Some of her thoughts must have communicated themselves to him for he followed her into the kitchen and said, "I was working."

She'd read his articles in the local paper. He wasn't meeting secret sources at midnight and bringing down governments; he wrote about local politics, and soft news features. She recalled him telling her that he also wrote speeches and penned annual reports. She couldn't imagine any of his subjects keeping him up all night. None of her business. She'd stupidly said she'd feed him, so she'd feed him. Then she'd send him back downstairs with a full belly and a suddenly free Friday night this week because there was no way she'd see him after this. "Right."

He drummed his fingers on her countertop, then reached out and placed a hand over hers. "Look. If I tell you something, will you keep it to yourself?"

She taught teenagers for a living. Did he think she was that gullible? "That would depend on the big secret."

He stared at her, indecision written all over his face. She couldn't tell whether he was making something up on the spot or working out whether he could confide in her. She pulled away and turned to slice the fresh loaf of Italian bread she'd bought earlier.

She stuck a basket of sliced bread in front of him and he devoured a piece.

"I'm writing a novel," he said as he worked on his second slice.

"A novel."

"Yes. And you are the first person I've told about it."

She remembered when Joe Stegna had told her he couldn't finish his Shakespeare essay because he was building a rocket ship in his basement. He'd worn just that look. She crossed her arms and gave Luke that don't-mess-with-me-I-can-give-you-an-F look. "And what is it called, this novel?"

He squirmed beneath her gaze. *Ha! Gotcha.*

"Prisons of the Mind." He moved around the kitchen counter behind her, opened her cutlery drawer and got out two knives, two forks and two spoons. "I know that title sucks, but it's just something to work with for now. What do you think?"

Anybody could pull a title out of the ether, was what she thought, remaining unconvinced that *Prisons of the Mind* didn't wear a D cup and moan a lot. "What's it about? Your book."

She opened the drawer beneath the one with the cutlery in it and passed him two place mats and two napkins. He lumbered back over to her small dining table and took his time setting it. "It's hard to talk about, you know?"

"I'll bet."

He set the table as though barely aware he was doing it. "I thought it was going to be a straight mystery. In fact, I didn't even start out to write a whole novel. I was only playing with some ideas. Then I got into this cop's head. He's the hero. But he's losing it. This case is sending him over the edge. He starts having difficulty finding the line between fantasy and reality, and meantime the killer starts messing with his mind. I haven't worked that part out yet. Nils is no dummy.''

''Nils?''

''That's the killer's name.''

''Nil. Nothing.''

He grinned at her as though she'd said the smartest thing he'd ever heard. ''Exactly. At some point Jenkins, the cop, isn't even sure the villain's real.'' His eyes were burning with enthusiasm and she now saw that she'd misjudged him. He *was* writing this novel.

She put the bread on the table between them and—what the hell, he already knew she'd planned to seduce him, he might as well know everything—pulled out the salad from the fridge. She handed him the bottle of Chianti, a corkscrew and a couple of wineglasses.

He flicked a glance at her but didn't say a word, for which she could have kissed him. He also turned off some of the lights and dragged a couple of candles over to the table so casually, she barely noticed.

''I know it sounds stupid. Everybody and his uncle thinks they can write a book, but—''

''I think it's fantastic. What a great way to stretch your mind and your creativity. And besides, you never know. It could be great. It sounds interesting already. I love psychological thrillers. Have you read…''

By the time the lasagna was ready they were well into a lively discussion about the books they liked, the writers they preferred, and he was admitting what he'd never told another soul, that he'd always dreamed of writing thrillers.

"How about you?" he asked as they dug into gelato. "Did you always want to be a teacher?"

She gazed at him across the table. Candlelight danced across his face, creating shadows and ridges, and reflected in his eyes. The ice cream was cold and sweet on her tongue. How amazing that after the complete debacle of her seduction plan, she should feel so utterly relaxed and able to talk about her life plans with this man. But, she found she could. "Yes. Always. I was the eldest child and we played school often, and I, of course, was always the teacher. My brothers and sister could all read and write by the time they started grade one."

"You must be a natural."

She shrugged. "I don't know about that. I'm pretty much learning as I go, but I do my best to keep it interesting. If I don't know anything about a subject I try to bring in an expert." She stopped and gasped, eyes widening as the obvious answer to her current dilemma stared back at her. "In fact, I'm doing a unit on journalism right now. I was planning to bring in a real live journalist. How'd you like to be our guest speaker?"

He glanced up and raised his brows. "Me?"

"Sure, why not?"

"I'm not a regular reporter, I work freelance."

"So what? That doesn't matter at all. In fact, you'll have a broader experience. Oh, please say you'll do it."

He looked really uncomfortable, and once again

she was forced to accept that for all his confident outward demeanor, he must be shy.

Luke stared across the table at Shari, wondering if she'd still be as eager for him to talk to her impressionable high school students if she knew he freelanced for other publications under the Lance Flagstaff pseudonym. If she knew, for instance, that his last column for *Men's Monthly* was titled, "Get Her Off Every Time."

He took a deep drink of his wine, knowing if he weren't so damned tired he could probably come up with a decent excuse not to speak to her class. His head was starting to feel as though it was full of thick, wet cement and the wine was making it set. He really needed sleep.

But, if there was a woman in the world he owed a favor, that woman was Shari.

Much as he'd been trying to push it to the back of his mind, the vision of her naked in candlelight would stay with him forever. He didn't think he'd ever seen anything so beautiful. The way he was going, chances weren't great he'd ever see her naked again, but damn it he was going to do his level best.

She was still looking at him expectantly and he knew he owed her. As long as no one knew he was also Lance Flagstaff there wasn't any danger he'd be accused of corrupting young minds. So he shrugged. "If you really want me to, then sure. My schedule's flexible. Let me know when the class times are and we'll work something out."

Her full lips parted on a warm smile. "Thanks, Luke. I really appreciate it."

There was a pause and his eyes felt so heavy he

knew he had to go before he added to his suave image by falling asleep in the dregs of his gelato. He stumbled to his feet. "Can I help you with the dishes?"

"No thanks, I've got it." She rose, headed toward her front door, opened it for him and edged back into the no-goodnight-kiss zone.

He turned to her. "Thanks for dinner."

"You're welcome." The atmosphere was suddenly strained and once more he could kick himself for his earlier foolishness. He didn't want this promising relationship to end because of an unfortunate experience with low blood sugar.

Her lips were slightly pinched and he felt the weight of awkwardness pressing on him. There must be something he could say to relieve it.

"Well," she said, "good night."

Oh, hell. Being an idiot hadn't killed him yet. They had to get beyond this. "So, am I ever going to see you naked again?"

Anger and a touch of hurt sparked in her eyes. "Not in this—"

He cut her off before she could finish, knowing he didn't want her making claims that he had no intention of letting her keep. He grabbed her shoulders and pulled her to him, kissing her hard to cut off her words, then softening his lips until her squeak of protest turned into a sigh.

He took his time to savor her softness and to feel her body's resistance slowly, slowly, melt. It wasn't easy and it went beyond technique, to a deeper level of communication, where he was telling her how much he wanted her with his lips, his tongue, letting her feel his body's arousal as he pulled her tight against him.

He pulled away slowly, enjoying the slightly stunned expression on her flushed face. If he weren't so far beyond tired that he'd make a worse fool of himself if he attempted to take her to bed now, he'd do just that. She was so ripe and womanly and so exactly what he needed at this moment.

She whispered slowly, as though the word was a playing card she'd forgotten she was holding. "Lifetime."

"Don't count on it," he said and left.

9

"AND THEN WHAT?" Therese was practically falling off her chair as she listened to Shari's story. They were in the library, supposedly working on lesson plans, but in reality gossiping behind their books just as the senior girls were doing behind the stacks.

Shari felt her face heating as she glanced around to make sure they couldn't be overheard. "And then he fainted."

Therese's shout of laughter caused instant silence as every student in the vicinity turned to stare at a teacher breaking the sacred silence of the library. It took her a few minutes to get herself under control so she could splutter, "Didn't I tell you it was a bad idea to get involved with that man?"

"Yes. You did. But you should have seen how embarrassed he was after it happened." In spite of herself she had to smile at the memory of him trying to insist he hadn't fainted.

"Hmm. I hope you gave him a piece of your mind when you threw him out."

"I gave him dinner."

"What?" Therese's explosive whisper sounded like a pot scrubber in action on the filthiest pot.

Shari lifted her shoulders helplessly, wishing she could explain the odd mix of feelings Luke inspired—

lust, nurturing, eye-rolling at his cluelessness, feeling flattered by his obvious attraction and frustrated at his inability to get past first base. He was an awfully good first baseman, though, which gave her hope that in time…

"Tell me you're ditching those stupid Friday-night sessions of yours," Therese almost groaned.

"I am a great teacher, and he's a student failing a really basic life skill. No, I'm not ditching the Fridays, I'm going to help him learn to be a great lover."

"You're crazy, woman."

Maybe she was crazy, but she knew she had the patience and skills to help Luke. And a tiny selfish part of her knew she'd be teaching him exactly how to please her. What wasn't great about that? "He's going to speak to my juniors about working as a reporter. You could meet him."

"Oh, there's something to look forward to. A guy who passes out at the sight of a woman's body." Therese shook her head.

To get her friend's mind off Luke's shortcomings, Shari said, "Hey, I heard Mr. Masters is leaving the school." Mr. Masters was the boys' baseball coach and one of the phys ed teachers.

"Yeah. His wife got transferred to Florida so they're moving."

"I wonder who'll take his place?"

"Do what I do. Picture a sixty-year-old married guy with bad breath. That way you're never disappointed."

"I think he's shy."

Therese stared at her. "We don't even know who it's going to be yet."

"No. I mean, Luke. I think he's shy. Now I'm wondering if he can handle a classful of smart-mouthed teenagers."

"Now she thinks of it." The first bell rang for the next class. Therese picked up her books and rose. "Tell him to eat before he comes. And warn the girls in class to cover up. A little cleavage or some belly button and he's likely to drop dead on the classroom floor."

Shari gathered her own things, knowing her gab session with Therese had earned her an extra hour of lesson planning tonight. She also had to have a strategy in place for when Luke came to her class. She didn't think he'd pass out, but it was probably best if she was prepared with planned questions for him and maybe a handout for the kids in case he was hopeless.

He'd seemed the perfect candidate when they were eating dinner, and so enthusiastic about his book that she'd gone with her gut and invited him as a speaker. Now she wasn't so sure about her judgment.

She wasn't so sure about a lot of things. Such as where he'd learned to kiss like that, and if he was a naturally good kisser, why wasn't he an instinctively good lover? Maybe he was and he simply lacked confidence. Maybe somewhere along the line an awful woman had really done a number on him. Regardless, she was determined to do her best to give him the confidence and skill he needed.

When she got home she was still trying to work out a more subtle strategy than surprising Luke with her naked body. She checked her mail. There was nothing *for* Luke. There was, however, something *from* him.

Her eyebrows rose and she wondered if it was a note of apology. Her stomach felt kind of squirmy. She hoped he hadn't penned something embarrassing. But, as it turned out, there wasn't a word about the other night. What she was holding was an outline of his planned talk to her class. The computer printout had subheads in the form of questions, which she quickly scanned.

Where do stories come from? How does a story go from idea to print? Who? What? When? Where? Why? Now let's write a news story. He'd scribbled a note at the bottom of the printout. "No promises, but if any of the students are interested we might be able to get a tour of the newspaper offices. Maybe one or two of them want to write a feature and I'd work with them to get it published. Your thoughts?"

Her thoughts: she wanted to kiss him. Right now.

Her students would slouch and mumble and make gagging noises about a field trip, but they'd probably love a tour of the newspaper. And a chance for a byline in a real newspaper would be a big motivator for a couple of the more studious kids.

Yes, she definitely wanted to kiss Luke. She'd been doing her level best not to think of the steamy one they'd shared and how good she'd felt in his arms. How good he'd felt half-naked rubbing against her on their hike. But she no sooner got warm and gooey thinking of those moments than the picture of him toppling to her rug while she'd stood there naked and mortified hijacked her memory.

If Luke wanted to get her naked again, he'd better memorize that damned book of his, because it was going to take every technique known to man to get her out of her clothes.

She stood in the lobby, clutching his notes for her class. She stared up at the high ceiling of the foyer as though inspiration might be found in the Art Deco light fixture, but inspiration wasn't hanging from the ceiling.

AFTER SLEEPING like the dead Monday night, Luke woke midmorning to the knowledge that he was screwed. And not in a good way. Far from masquerading as a Total Moron, he'd *become* one in front of a woman he wanted more than he'd ever wanted anyone.

Playing shamelessly on her request that he speak to her class, he'd gone out of his way to add some pizzazz to his guest appearance at her high school by browbeating and begging his editor into letting him bring a school tour through. The price for the favor was taking an assignment to write a feature about a breast-feeding club.

He'd thought the editor was joking, but the photos were already done, the feature slotted for the weekend edition and the *pregnant, female* writer who'd originally been assigned the piece had gone into labor prematurely and was currently in hospital. With a newborn.

Excuses. But he'd said yes so the editor would allow Shari's kids to submit something—anything—to the paper.

Still, the price had been a hefty one. An article about breasts now, and he was your man. But breast-feeding? He felt a little squirrelly at the thought of being trapped in a room with a bunch of postpartum women. He'd heard stories.

What if they'd all had terrible labors and turned on him as a representative of all males who make females suffer? They could tear him to bits. There ought to be danger pay attached to the assignment.

He'd tried to get a phone interview, but the editor wasn't having any of it. Luke had to show up at this breast-feeding meeting next Wednesday night, then write his feature Thursday.

The only strategy he could imagine to get him through it was to imagine it was Shari's breasts they were talking about and him doing the sucking.

When he heard the knock on his door, he knew it had been worth it to promise to write about lactating women. The lure of a newspaper tour and possible article may not have drawn Shari irresistibly to him, but at least she hadn't canceled their deal as he'd feared. He'd have preferred that it was his manly magnificence that had her banging on the door, except there was nothing manly or magnificent about his recent behavior. Maybe he could write a sequel to his book—*Normal Guy to Total Moron in Two Weeks or Less.*

He opened his door. As he'd suspected, Shari stood there. She hadn't even stopped at her own apartment after work. Her schoolbag was still in her arms, along with her mail and his ideas for her class.

"Hey," she said.

"Hey, yourself." He opened the door wider and she hesitated before entering.

"It's okay," he assured her with weak humor, "I ate breakfast and lunch."

"Oh." She brushed at the air with his printout, laughing in a breathless spurt. "Don't be silly. I only came to thank you for this."

"Do you think it's the right approach?"

She beamed at him, and he wondered why none of his high school teachers had ever looked so good. "It's perfect. Absolutely perfect. I've tried every year to get the newspaper to give us a tour. How did you pull it off?"

He shrugged, trying not to think of the ordeal ahead of him next Wednesday night. "The editor owed me a favor."

She gazed at him quizzically. "Now I guess I owe you one."

"No." He took a step toward her, wanting to touch, knowing he couldn't. "No. I…you were great last night. You fed me dinner, listened to me ramble on about my novel." Unable to stop himself, he reached out and touched a lock of her hair where it curled like a question mark against her shoulder. "I had a good time."

She looked like she was fighting a smile. "Me, too."

He felt something crackle between them and he'd bet anything she was reliving their kiss just as he was.

After a stunned second of staring at him, she blinked a couple of times. "Well, I should be—"

"Did you work out today?" he interrupted, knowing he didn't want their contact to be so brief.

"I'm up to seventy-eight sit-ups in the morning and twenty push-ups."

"Pretty good. Speaking as your personal trainer,

I'd say you need to come for a run and then I'll reward you with pizza.''

"I hate running."

He shrugged. "It's your wedding."

She bit her lip, and he watched her try to decide whether to take another chance on him or not. "I'll meet you in front of the building in fifteen minutes."

Relief flooded him, but he kept his voice casual. "What kind of pizza do you like?"

"Huh?"

"I'll order it now and we'll pick it up when we go by."

"You're good at this. I don't care."

"Fully loaded. We'll run fast."

She chuckled and let herself out the door.

He was out front waiting within ten minutes, and she wasn't far behind. She was always prompt. He liked that about her. In fact, there was a lot to like about Shari. Including how good she looked in gray cotton running shorts, a white T-shirt and sneakers. They stretched a bit and then set off. He let her set the pace, guiding her on his easier three-mile course.

Even though he was a fairly bogus personal trainer, he still kept an eye on her, making sure she didn't overdo it. Her hair was pulled back in a ponytail and the curls bounced and tumbled as she jogged. She wasn't a sprinter, but she had a nice, easy pace. He relaxed, figuring out she wasn't planning to push herself to try to impress him, then grinned to himself. Why on earth would she try to impress him?

"Hey, Luke," called Simon, who was out watering the tiered stacks of flowering plants in front of his Asian grocery on the corner.

"Hi, Simon."

"He's just sent his second son off to college," he told Shari. "Watch the next curb, it's a long drop."

"You see the world in a different way when you're not driving all the time," she said, half to herself.

"That's the fun of living here. All the life is outside. For a guy like me who works at home a lot of the time, that's important."

They left the street and crossed to jog around Volunteer Park. It had rained earlier in the day and the air still felt damp and misty.

By the time they made the return leg, he was feeling pleasantly loose and Shari had the pink glow of health in her cheeks and a light sheen of perspiration across her cheekbones.

He jogged into the pizza place and jogged out again with the large square box, making her laugh. He'd long ago learned the trick of putting the whole thing, including the tip, on his credit card in advance so he didn't have to carry money.

"I'm starving," she said when they entered his apartment, the warm pizza box sending fragrant, teasing steam into the air.

"Me, too," he admitted. And his body wasn't hungry for just pizza.

He flipped on the news while she washed up, then picked up the remote control to turn it off when she returned, but she stopped him. "No. This is good. I didn't have time to read the paper this morning."

So they sat side by side on his couch, the cardboard box on the low pine table in front of them, and munched pizza while they watched the news. It was surprisingly relaxed and, while he'd have preferred another, very intimate workout, sitting here sharing dinner and catching up on news was nice, too. Friendly.

He realized with a shock that they were becoming friends. Which was odd. Apart from his sisters, he didn't have many women friends.

When the news ended, a sitcom rerun came on and they both shook their heads. Using his universal remote, he flipped off the TV and hit the CD button. He couldn't remember what was in there, but it turned out to be vintage Rod Stewart. Pretty good date music, he decided.

She sat with one leg curled under her and, without the TV to distract them, awareness hovered in the air. She reached for another slice of pizza, more for something to do, he suspected, than that she really wanted it.

As she raised it to her lips, a plump slice of mushroom toppled off the triangle and plopped onto her inner thigh.

"Oops," she said, and reached for the mushroom slice.

He stopped her while lust curled in his belly.

"I'll get it," he said softly. And he did, using not his hands, but his lips and teeth. The skin of her thigh was soft, smooth, and so sensitive she giggled as he lifted the mushroom off her flesh with his teeth. He ate without tasting, then lapped at the spot of tomato sauce with his tongue. Her giggle turned into a sigh as he let his tongue roam. She tasted warm, a little salty from the run. While his mouth was busy, his fingers traced the hem of her loose gray shorts.

When he'd written *Sex for Total Morons,* he'd expanded the first part from a published article he'd once written and called "Four Dates to the Bedroom." Of course, a lot of women didn't take four dates, but he liked that getting-to-know-you time, the anticipation and the buildup. He thought of it as the foreplay before the foreplay. So, if he were willing to stretch the definition of date, dinner at Shari's had meant he'd finished chapter four. Which meant he was free and clear to work his way to chapter five. He liked chapter five. Not as much as chapter six, but five was good.

"What are you doing?" Her breathy tone had him hardening. He heard the message behind the words, and it sounded like *yes, please.* Chapter five, here we come!

"The mushroom traveled," he said against her skin. He nudged the edge of her shorts up with his nose and followed with his tongue, but she stopped him, shoving a hand against his forehead.

"I need a shower," she all but wailed.

As if he cared. What was a little healthy perspiration between friends—or better still—lovers, but he'd been with enough women to know better than to argue. He skimmed his lips up the outside of her shorts and pushed up her shirt. Fortunately, she wasn't as squeamish about him kissing her belly.

She had a great stomach. A layer of softness over taut muscle. He lapped and nuzzled her there while his fingers traveled the path his tongue was forbidden.

He traced the edge of her panties and felt the tension already building in her; it upped his own tension by a mile. He slipped his hand under the elastic, petted the soft curls and reached down and there she was—hot, pouty and already slick.

"Oh," she moaned softly as he began to caress her, rubbing the outer folds and feathering over the tight bud at the center of everything.

"Do you like it like this?" he whispered.

"Oh, mmm. Yes." He pushed a finger inside her slowly and felt everything contract as she gasped. Even the muscles of her belly tightened against his lips. Part of him wanted to kiss her breasts and mouth, but it was kind of a rush being in on the action down here, so he stayed where he was, his tongue teasing her belly and sweeping as far as her hipbones. He was able to keep an eye on the way her pelvis began to thrust against his hand.

He didn't think she knew she was doing it, but her hands were clutching his hair, pulling so his scalp stung as she closed in on ecstasy. Her breath rushed in and out of her lungs as he worked her closer and closer to the edge. He couldn't stop himself, he needed to watch her face, to kiss her mouth, so he moved until he was lying beside her, perched awkwardly on the edge of the couch.

Her eyes were closed, her head thrown back, her cheeks wonderfully flushed, mouth open on a sigh. He kissed her, tasting spicy pizza and hot woman. She was still clutching his hair, helpless little pants driving him crazy as he made love to her mouth, mimicking the movements of his thrusting fingers. Her body clenched, tighter and tighter in a hot, wet fist, and then he sent her over the edge, sucking her cry of release into his mouth.

He kissed her until it was clear he was doing all

the kissing and she was lying there, rigid. He fought an urge to roll his eyes. What was this all about?

"I shouldn't have…let that happen. I'm supposed to be planning a lesson." She glanced at him, half shy. His muscles and gravity were fighting a tug-of-war to keep him on the couch. "Besides, you don't look very comfortable."

She had no idea how uncomfortable he was, but he had a damn good idea of how he could rid himself of the sudden buildup of tension. Maybe he'd give her a little hint. "I have a nice big bed in the other room."

She wrinkled her nose. "We're all sweaty from running."

He grinned down at her. "We'll get sweatier."

She chuckled, then shook her head, resting her palm against his cheek. "I don't… I have to think about this."

Yesterday, she'd tried to seduce him, now she was having second thoughts. What a difference a fainting spell could make in a guy's sex life. If he ever updated his book, he'd have to put a chapter in there about the importance of regular meals.

10

"REMEMBER TO BRING in your newspaper article ideas for next class." Shari tried to be heard over the drone of the school bell indicating the end of the day and the chatting, giggling and scraping of chairs against lino as the students reverted instantly into escape-from-class mode.

In truth, she was just as glad as they were to escape. She was going shopping. It was time she started looking for a great outfit for B.J.'s wedding; besides, the added distraction would be good for her. She felt as though she had to keep reminding herself of the wedding and the deal she and Luke had made. Anything to stop her contemplating the other night.

What had she been thinking?

She hadn't been thinking at all. That was clearly the trouble.

If she'd considered the implications of playing sexy games on Luke's couch for a nanosecond she'd have gone home long before the man's hands found their way into her panties. For a normally slow, shy guy he'd been remarkably slick about sneaking under her guard and, once he was touching her...

She squirmed, forcing herself to recite "Ode to Autumn," as though the few students who hadn't already bolted might find their volatile teenage hormones ignited by her steamy thoughts.

She was thinking about Keats with grim determination when a knock on her open door had her turning. Her mouth dropped open. "Therese?"

She'd often heard the expression, "You look like you've seen a ghost," but her friend looked more as though she'd just tripped over a bloody corpse. She was white, her eyes wild, and she clutched a yellow printed sheet in hands that shook. With a darting glance to the two students who were chatting at the back of Shari's class, Therese said in a jumpy voice that didn't come close to sounding as casual as the words, "Can I see you for a second?"

"Of course." She raised her voice. "Okay, Myra and Brian. I need to lock up now. See you Friday."

She got a grunt from one and a "See ya" from the other, as they left through the back door. Shari hastened to lock it after them, then dragged Therese in the front door and locked it behind her.

"What is it?"

Therese thrust the badly crinkled yellow sheet at her. It was damp where she'd gripped it and Shari assumed her friend's palms had been sweating. She glanced at the paper, recognizing the announcement of the replacement phys ed teacher. A fellow named Brad Koslowski from a school across town was replacing Mr. Masters. All the teachers had received a copy in their office mail slots this morning. She looked closer at Therese's sheet, searching for some scribbled message. There was none. She flipped the paper over but the back of the sheet was blank.

"I don't know what I'm looking for," she finally admitted.

"It's *him!*" Therese flapped her hand at the paper.

"Him who?"

"The man I was telling you about who made me believe in homely men."

Shari gasped as recollection hit her. "You mean, the short, weedy balding guy with the Olympic-medal tongue?"

Therese groaned and sank her head into her hands. "I never thought I'd see him again. How dare he come to my school after he dumped me for some Minnesota sauna girl."

Shari remembered now. Therese had let herself fall for the less-than-perfect looking man because of his inner qualities, and what did his evolved inner self do but dump her for a tall Swedish centerfold type. "Oh, honey, that's awful. But he's the one who should be suffering, not you. Right?"

"Right." Therese raised her head and a little of her usual sparkle was back. "Right! Give me that." She snatched the seriously mauled paper out of Shari's hand, scrunched it into a ball and tossed it in the trash.

"Have you seen him?" Shari asked.

Therese shook her head. "But it's bound to happen. I bet he doesn't even remember I teach here. Self-centered egomaniac. *Cochon. Imbecile!*" Therese, whose English was flawless, fell back into her native French in times of stress, and even her English became accented. Shari had never seen her lose her English over a guy before. She had it bad.

"There are times when a girl has to turn to chocolate," Shari said, thinking a good sugar and cocoa binge was probably just what her friend needed, along with a chance to rail and rant to a sympathetic listener. Because Therese was going to have to pull herself together and accept that she and Brad the Tongue were going to be working together whether she liked it or not.

"Oui. C'est vrai."

"Um, if we're going to get very far with this, you're going to have to speak English."

Therese clapped a hand to her mouth. "Sorry." Then, with a determined nod, she said, "Have you ever had a chocolate martini? I've discovered a new place. The Chocolate Bar."

Somehow, Shari didn't think they served her kind of chocolate bar, or that she was going to get a lot of shopping done tonight, but she had a friend in need, who looked as though she'd require someone to make sure she got home okay at the end of the evening.

They both went home to change clothes and then went to the funky martini bar Therese had recently discovered. Since she hated martinis and, anyway, one of them needed to keep their wits, Shari settled on a single glass of white wine and they spent a good hour trashing men in general and Brad in particular. She'd never seen Therese like this before, and the obvious reason finally dawned.

"You fell in love with him, didn't you?"

A stream of French, too rapid and passionate for Shari to follow, issued forth while Therese's eyes snapped and her hands gesticulated madly. Shari let the torrent flow, understanding the sentiments underneath the incomprehensible words. At last Therese wound down, her eyes filled with tears and she whispered, "Yes. I did."

Shari had intended to tell Therese about Luke's latest exploits, and the surprising way he'd gone from acting like Mr. Shy to moving on her so fast that she was crying out in ecstasy almost before she'd realized where his hands were. A close girlfriend's take on the whole situation might help her sort out her feelings, but she couldn't do it. Not while Therese was in crisis.

She had no idea what chapter they were on in Luke's how-to book, or even if they were still following the curriculum. The episode on his couch the other night felt like a whole different book.

From where they were, it wasn't far to full-fledged sex. Was she ready for that with Luke? She'd thought she was after their hiking trip, but what with the fainting and the mixed messages he seemed to send her, she wasn't certain. Looking at Therese bravely holding back tears, she had to accept that sex made her vulnerable.

Shari couldn't allow a man into her body in a casual way. Maybe she was old-fashioned, but to her intimacy mattered.

The more she grew to like her downstairs neighbor as a friend, the more dangerous sleeping with him might turn out to be. Sure, she could help him become a wonderful lover, but what would she do when he was ready to graduate from her school?

As the hours ticked by, their regular Friday night lesson/date was starting to loom like a dentist's appointment.

FRIDAY. Luke savored the word as he planned the evening in his mind. Friday had become his favorite day of the week. This one was the day they'd make love.

"About Friday," he said when he called to make the arrangements. "Why don't you come to my place and I'll cook?"

He could call it dinner. He could invite her in to play Parcheesi. Didn't matter. They both knew what he meant. In this case, dinner was the appetizer. He wanted to tease her by telling her he was planning to serve a double batch of oysters, but he didn't suppose a guy who needed a book like *Sex for Total Morons* would be so flippant about sex he'd make jokes about aphrodisiacs.

Besides, Shari sounded strained on the phone. In truth, he didn't feel as calm and casual as he normally did when planning an evening that was destined to end in bed. For some reason he couldn't fathom, this time was different.

"Well, um…" she sputtered.

Please don't be trying to think up an excuse to cancel our date. *Please,* he silently pleaded with her.

After a long pause she said, "Do you want me to bring dessert?"

If things went according to plan, she was going to be dessert. This was his night to seduce her into his bed through food and a few other tips outlined in his book.

"No," he said. "I've got it under control." Thanks to the Danish bakery he jogged by most days.

He'd flipped through chapter six earlier and had found himself becoming stirred reading the chapter he'd written. He was planning to ease Shari into the chapter as though the pages were satin sheets—although he didn't own satin sheets. Good old navy-blue cotton did the job for him. He always felt if he was doing the seducing correctly, a woman shouldn't notice what kind of sheets were on the bed—or if there were sheets, or whether she was even on a bed.

Of course, since he'd met Shari, his confidence had been knocked down a mile or two. With his luck of late, he'd probably burst his appendix on the way to the bedroom. With a suggestive see-you-later, he hung up and gave his belly a tentative poke. Everything seemed to be at peace, including his appendix. Only his libido was restless.

Oh, he had big plans for tonight. And, he realized, he could finally bring out those candles. Shari was definitely a candles-and-moonlight kind of woman. He ached to see her in both lights.

SHARI HUMMED along to Natalie Imbruglia, soft and sultry on her CD, and slipped into a silky tank that clung where it touched. Her marathon exercise regime was definitely starting to show. She hadn't seen her triceps in so long she'd forgotten she owned a pair.

Her shoulders had a little more definition and her belly was definitely more taut. Her cheeks were a healthy pink and even her eyes glowed a richer brown than usual. Torn between hip-hugging pants and a tiny excuse of a skirt, she found the thought flitting through her head that she should pick the one that was easiest to remove in the heat of passion—then stopped.

Wait a minute. Whoa, girl.

Eyes narrowed now, she stared at herself in a new

light. Seduction was almost certainly on tonight's
menu, she suspected. She simply wasn't certain what
she intended to do about it. Sure, Luke was sexy, and
the more she got to know him, the more she liked
him, but she wanted the sex on her terms. Based on
the other night, they were past chapter four and she'd
fulfilled her part of the bargain. She might teach Luke
about loving a woman properly and she might not.
She hadn't decided yet.

With a frustrated oath, she dragged the silky tank
off and tossed it onto the bed.

She stood there in her bra and panties and, in that
second, saw Luke's eyes roll back in his head as he
crashed to the floor of her apartment. She shuddered.
No way she was putting herself through that again.

Digging into her closet she flipped right by her fun
clothes to the clothing hinterland in the hard-to-reach
section where the boring, unflattering and out-of-style
garments stuck together like stale slices of sandwich
meat. She peeled a red velour jumpsuit away from a
designer knockoff that wouldn't fool anyone and realized she was seriously in need of a closet purge.

Deeper she went until she caught sight of a large
expanse of denim, and nodded. Perfect. Huffing, she
maneuvered the long, loose denim skirt out of her
closet and paired it with a baggy, white cotton sweater
from the bottom of her sweater pile.

Shoving herself into the billows of fabric, she had
the dubious satisfaction of knowing there was no way
this outfit could incite lust in Luke or anyone else.
Once again she checked herself out in the long mirror
and grimaced. After tonight she was going to chuck

both the sweater and the skirt, along with the other horror stories in the back of her closet.

If she and Luke were going to become intimate, and it was a big if, it would be on her terms and according to her timetable.

Even so, she couldn't quite suppress the shudder of anticipation as she walked down to his floor and knocked on his door.

He opened it and she blinked. She'd never seen him in anything but well-worn casual clothes before. Tonight he wore black linen dress pants, shiny black leather loafers and a black shirt of a weave so fine she wanted to touch it. The neck was open and just a hint of chest hair teased her, reminding her of how it had felt to rub her naked chest against his. Tonight he'd dressed. For her.

She felt a shiver of delight at the implied compliment, then made the mistake of looking right into his eyes. She froze. His green eyes were always a little sleepy, as though nothing in life was worth getting too worked up over, but tonight they were sharp and keen, slicing through all the airy decisions she'd made earlier.

These weren't the eyes of a laid-back guy who didn't know how to please a woman. These were the eyes of a predator, one who would take control of her body, of her will, and bend her to his.

She sucked in a startled breath and blinked. And the impression was gone as though she'd imagined it. Back was the Luke she knew. He was running his gaze over her outfit and a quick gleam of humor made her suspect he knew exactly why she was wearing the closest thing to a burka she could find.

"Come in," he said.

"Thanks." She presented him with a bottle of chilled white wine. "I wasn't sure. But it seemed kind of warm today for red."

"This is perfect," he said, but something in his tone made her feel the way the fly would after giving the spider a present—as though she were being toyed with before being eaten.

She entered the apartment and the feeling of strangeness didn't leave her. He had a small round table set for two outside on his patio. Near the door, there was a tub of herbs, which impressed her, and there were metal lanterns containing candles. Once they were settled with glasses of wine, he flipped off the lights inside his apartment, and she found her sense of displacement growing stronger.

The sun had already set and there was only a sliver of moon. The air was still warm from the unseasonably hot day, but in the dark, with a hint of fresh herbs scenting the air, she felt as though she were in the south of France or Italy.

With her companion seemingly so mysterious and this patio so visually disconnected from the rest of the world, a turmoil of sensations stirred inside her— mystery, uncertainty and the hot, enticing spice of desire.

In an attempt to drown that desire, she gulped wine too quickly and chattered manically about how excited the kids were that Luke was coming to talk to them next week. "I decided to assign them all an article to write after you've done your session. We'll go through them as a class and vote on the best ones.

Perhaps the best three. And then, if it's all right with you, you could pick the winner."

"I think I could pick a winner," he said, his voice seeming surprisingly deep all of a sudden.

"Thank you." She picked up her glass to drink more wine and discovered it was empty. Wow. That was fast. She checked to see if he used really small glasses, but they were a generous size. She must be thirsty.

As she put down her empty glass, he rose to fill it. "Are you hungry?"

Hungry. She was so hungry every part of her felt empty and screaming for fulfillment. Why did he have to have all the appearance and attributes of a sexually exciting man and always fall apart at the critical moment? Anyway, for all the nuance she heard in his voice, he was obviously talking about food, and if she was smart she'd switch to drinking water.

"I'm ready for dinner," she said carefully. "And may I have a glass of water?"

"Sure. I'll be just a minute."

In less than a minute he'd filled her wineglass and set a glass of water in front of her. He disappeared inside and in no more than ten minutes, reappeared with two plates. Lighting a couple more candles on the table, he illuminated a dinner that could have come from any five-star restaurant.

"Mmm. Tuna?" she guessed, staring at the steak-like piece of fish, with some kind of vegetable salsa on top, complete with rice and spears of baby asparagus.

"Energy food," he answered. "Great when you're working out a lot."

"Is that my personal trainer talking?"

His eyes glowed, enigmatic and devilish against his black clothing. "Something like that."

Was there a technique in his stupid book about talking in nothing but double meanings and obscure statements? She should find that thing and burn it. She felt as though she were being nudged along, page by page to the chapter of no return and she didn't like it. She was the teacher, damn it. She was supposed to be in charge.

Still, the fresh tuna was incredible, dense and flavorful, and Luke's conversation seemed a lot less weird once they tucked into their dinner.

Once she'd told him a bit more about her day at school and thrown in a cute-kid anecdote or two, she asked him what he'd been up to lately.

He seemed to squirm a little in his seat, then said, "I was working on an article."

"For the local paper?" She'd have to watch for it and take it into class.

"No, for a magazine."

"Really?" She didn't recall him telling her about magazine work. "That's exciting. What kind of magazine? Is it a feature?"

He cleared his throat, reached for the nearly empty wine bottle and topped up their nearly full glasses—which he'd topped about two seconds ago. "It's a men's magazine. I do some work for them."

He was clearly uncomfortable talking about it so she let the topic drop. It was probably *Matchbook Collecting Monthly,* or something really lame. She respected his right not to have to tell her everything he wrote for money. "How's the novel coming?" she asked to guide the conversation onto safer ground.

"It's great. Now I've got it mapped out and the characters are clear in my head, it's as if they keep talking to me. I think I'm going insane myself. There are voices in my head. I kid you not."

"What do they say?" She was mildly amused, but also fascinated. She'd never known anyone who'd written a novel before. Well, except for her brother, Sam, who used to write the adventures of SuperSam as a kid, complete with hand-drawn cartoons.

"They don't talk to me. They talk to each other. It's kind of spooky, but cool. This morning the psychiatrist told the hero she wouldn't marry him. Of course, I pretty much knew she'd refuse, but she did it right when the poor guy was hurting. He needed to be strong and her rejection weakened him. Now the killer's closing in."

She shivered at the intense expression on his face. She could tell Luke had disappeared into his story world. It was fascinating. "Will she change her mind?" she asked softly.

"Hmm? Who?"

"The woman. The psychiatrist. Will she change her mind and marry him in the end? That's the kind of book I like. I'm a sucker for a happy ending."

He shook his head and in the flickering candlelight she saw his lip curl in derision. "No. She won't make that mistake."

"Mistake? But he needs her." She leaned forward, feeling, from what Luke had told her about the book, as though she half knew these people. "She helps him stay strong. Without her, he's too vulnerable."

"You're a romantic, Shari. People have to be strong on their own. It's the only way to get through life."

"Well, I admit to being a romantic," she said, a little stung at his easy dismissal of marriage. "But it's better than being a cynic."

"Cynics don't lose their illusions."

She thought of her friend Therese. "Most cynics I know are romantics who have lost their illusions. Is that what happened to you, Luke?"

The sound the metal legs of his chair made when they scratched against the cement-floored balcony was like that of a match being lit. "We're talking about characters in a book."

"That cynical-loner attitude seems to be coming from you."

He shrugged and leaned back in his chair to stare at the curving glitter of moon and the few scattered stars. "Marriage isn't for me. Doesn't mean it doesn't work for some people."

Sadness trickled through her. His words were matter-of-fact, but she sensed his seeming nonchalance blocked a heap of pain. Somebody had hurt him, and hurt him bad.

"Ready for coffee and dessert?"

She hesitated. It was barely ten. She couldn't leave now. "I'm too full for dessert. I'll do the dishes while you make the coffee."

"Deal."

She rinsed and put the plates and cutlery in the dishwasher, realizing that Luke was a much neater cook than she was. Once the coffee had brewed, she hesitated about going back outside. But that couch brought back memories that gave her a hot combination of embarrassment and desire.

He took the decision away from her by saying, "Come on. I want to show you something."

Taking her hand, he led her toward a door. Since their apartments were identical, she knew what was behind it.

"That's your bedroom."

"I know. It's where I keep my computer. I was hoping you'd read the passage in my book that I told you about. Let me know if the psychiatrist's dialogue sounds like something a woman would say."

This was either the cheesiest excuse she'd ever heard to get a woman into his bedroom or he actually wanted her to read a bit of his novel, which was fascinating, and possibly a window into how Luke felt about women.

But did she really want to go into his bedroom?

11

SHARI DECIDED TO be perfectly grown-up and professional about the fact that Luke's desk was in his bedroom. She'd simply ignore the bed and see only the office part of the room. She really wanted a peek at the novel after hearing him talk about it. She was curious. Was it any good?

Her skirt felt as heavy as armor as they walked through the doorway. Of course, as in most bedrooms, his bed dominated the room. The duvet was navy-and-black plaid. Kind of Ralph-Lauren-meets-hunter's-sleeping-bag lining—very masculine. The pillow cases, and presumably the sheets, were also navy, but she got the feeling he hadn't tried to match them, it was more that he liked the color.

The bed and an old oak highboy were pushed off-center to make room for his office, such as it was—a black computer desk, a floor-to-ceiling bookcase and a file cabinet, all scrupulously neat. He was a lot tidier than she.

While she inspected his room, noting he had a lot of her favorite authors in his bookcase as well as reference books, grammar primers and dictionaries, he booted up his computer and called up the file of his novel. She glanced at the page total. "Wow. Three hundred pages."

"It's only a rough draft," he explained, his diffident side showing again.

She smiled at the back of his head, and noticed that his dark brown hair was starting to curl over his collar. He needed a haircut, but she sort of liked his unkempt style. It suited him.

"Here you go," he said. "It's just this scene." He stood and offered her the seat.

She took the computer chair and began to read.

Jenkins lit a cigarette from the butt of the one burning his fingers. He noted with casual contempt that both hands shook, hampering the simple procedure. Claire sat, still and composed, hands clasped on top of her prescription pad. He'd have to remind her to order him more sleeping pills.

"Say something, dammit. I asked you to marry me. If it's no, say so. Let's get it over with."

She stared at him, as cool and untouchable as the Madonnas in the cathedrals his ma dragged him to when he was a kid.

"It's no." He didn't have to remind her about the pills. She stared at him until he wanted to break something, then quietly wrote the prescription. Unlike all the other shrinks who'd treated him, she didn't scrawl illegible symbols on the pad, but took her time, writing in flowing cursive the full name of the drug and the amount of oblivion he could have.

When she held it out to him he tried to snatch it from her, but she stopped him, laying a hand against his cheek. ''I'm sorry.''

The funny thing was that, at the time, he believed her.

Shari continued reading, amazed at how quickly Luke's story pulled her in, even though the scene was from somewhere in the middle of the book. She read rapidly, immediately caught up in the dilemma of the troubled cop and his psychiatrist.

She was vaguely aware of Luke pacing behind her.

She read about ten pages before Luke's hand settled atop hers, stopping her. She glanced up to where he stood over her. ''That's it? That's all I can read?''

''Yeah. It's the part that's bothering me. What do you think?''

''I want to read more. This is only enough to tease me.''

''But is that how a woman would react? How, say, you would react?''

''If a man asked me to marry him, I hope I wouldn't be as cold. But since I don't know the rest of the story, it's hard to understand her motivation.''

She went back and read the opening of the scene again, slowly, seeing hints she'd missed on the first read. ''This isn't about her. It's all about him. Maybe that's why she's turned him down. Look at the way he describes her. He's not looking for a lover, he sees her as a maternal figure. He likens her to the Madonnas his mother took him to see. With the psychiatrist's desk and prescription pad, she represents authority. And what's he doing? Chain-smoking. He knows damn well you can't smoke in a hospital. He's being a naughty boy, pushing her away even as he needs her.''

"A mother figure?" Luke said in amazement.

"Well, that's the way I'm reading it. And I'm guessing she sees through him, too. Does she love him?" She shrugged. "Maybe. I haven't read enough. But I'm guessing he needs to love her as a man loves a woman, not as a child loves his mother or as a patient looks up to his shrink." She sent him a half smile. "He's a fascinating guy, Luke. Are you sure I can't read some more?"

He was smiling at her, white teeth gleaming, the cleft in his chin shadowed. "And you're a fascinating woman." Even as she opened her mouth to reply, he leaned forward, slipped a hand behind her head and covered her mouth with his.

A breathy murmur broke from her as she tried to remember why this was a bad idea. The feel of Luke's lips teasing hers, warm and sure, broke her concentration. Her mind might have some vague ideas about saying no, but her entire body was screaming, yes.

He swiveled the chair until her knees bumped his, then deepened the kiss. She threw her arms around his neck, pulling him against her. Whatever his other shortcomings, the man could surely kiss. In fact, the man tonight was totally unlike the man she knew. Except, of course, for the odd glimpse of vulnerability that reminded her he was there—like a homely undershirt peeking out from the neck of a designer shirt. He was Luke, the unsure man who fainted at the sight of her nakedness, and he was Luke, the man whose kisses made putty of her knees. She tried to pull him closer still until the chair gave a warning squeak.

He pulled back, green eyes so intent she shivered. Then he dipped and, putting a hand under her knees and another behind her shoulders, lifted her as though she weighed nothing.

She giggled with surprise and delight before the giggle changed to a whimper as he laid her on his bed. Now it was her turn to be uncertain.

Was she ready for this? What if it was terrible? What if he had some kind of awful performance anxiety, what if…?

He kissed her again and joined her on the bed, turning her so that they were on their sides, facing each other. It was quickly apparent that he wasn't suffering any performance anxiety at the moment. He was rock-hard in all the right places, snugging against her and nudging all her softest parts.

Dimly she realized they'd been on this path since the first day they'd exchanged mail. Plus, she knew herself. She was a kind and decent person. If Luke had a problem she could help him with, she would.

Her lips curved against his as she thought about what a good teacher she was. Taking an inept man and turning him into an exquisite lover was pretty heady stuff. She felt her power and decided to have some fun with this most intimate lesson of all.

"Touch me," she whispered.

"Where?" Uncertain or teasing? She couldn't decide and didn't care.

She rose to sitting and yanked off her sweater, which was going to Goodwill the first chance she got. She felt as if she'd been walking around in a bedspread.

She watched his face as his gaze roamed her torso,

his eyes crinkling with humor as they took in her lacy pink bra from the latest Victoria's Secret catalog.

"What?" she asked, a bit incensed. He had the oddest reactions of any man she'd ever known.

"After the sweater and skirt, I thought maybe you had corsets and a girdle under there."

She chuckled softly and decided to crawl out of the six-man denim tent.

At the sight of her matching pink panties, he sighed. "I was going crazy wondering what you were wearing under those clothes."

He reached out to trace the edge of each lacy bra cup in a sweeping vee over her breasts. The slight abrasion of his finger on her sensitive flesh sent delicious shudders running through her. It was hard to tell in the dim light of his desk lamp, but he didn't look pale or close to passing out. Still, she thought if she kept his mind off her imminent nakedness it might help him prepare to actually make love with her. If they even got that far tonight. She was determined to show patience and care with him.

"I'm going to donate them both to charity tomorrow," she said, a shade huskily since he'd just leaned forward and taken her nipple in his mouth, silky bra and all.

He pulled back to stare at her. "Are you kidding? That's one of the sexiest outfits I've ever seen. I was going crazy imagining your body underneath all that…fabric."

She chuckled, realizing her plan to appear totally sexless had basically backfired. "You are a very strange man, do you know that?"

"Trust me. You'd look sexy wrapped in garbage bags."

He leaned forward to her breasts again, but she stopped him. "Now you take your shirt and pants off."

Without any finesse or teasing whatsoever, he dragged his shirt off, unbuckled his pants, kicked off his shoes and yanked off his slacks and socks in under about ten seconds. He rose and turned back to her wearing nothing but black briefs. She had only a moment to admire the utter beauty of his body before he was beside her again.

Where he'd seemed content to toy with her before, he now seemed barely controlled. His chest rose and fell rapidly, and his erection nudged insistently when he rolled against her once more. "I want you so much," he murmured against her throat.

At his words, she realized the same was true for her. She did want him, and badly. She couldn't remain still. Her pelvis seemed to have its own agenda, rocking against his hardness, teasing, damn near begging to be filled. He plunged a hand into her panties and touched her, but it wasn't nearly enough. With a strangled moan, she grabbed the waistband and dragged the silky restriction off.

She reached for his briefs, but he'd beaten her to it, tearing them off before tossing them over his shoulder.

She checked him out and her mouth went dry. He looked even more fabulous naked than he did clothed. His erection was big and bold. She wanted to touch him to see if he was as hard as he appeared.

His fingers were fumbling with the bra she'd forgotten she was still wearing, and she wasn't wearing it for long. "God, you're beautiful," he whispered, once more kissing her breasts.

His hand slid between her legs and, before she was beyond rational thought, she grabbed at his wrist. "Luke. Do you have condoms?" She had some upstairs, but getting dressed and trundling up to her place was a mood breaker if ever there was one.

Instead of speaking, he reached for his night table, opened the drawer, dug around without looking and pulled out two square packages.

She was so excited that they might actually get there this time that she threw her arms around him and pulled him on top of her. She'd tried to restrain herself, half certain some disaster would fall, but now it seemed all lights were green. She wanted him inside her and she wanted him now.

She couldn't get enough of him, touch enough of his warm, smooth skin taut over tough muscle. She felt herself softening and opening for him, aching to be penetrated.

They kissed hungrily, crazily, until she was dizzy from lack of breath and anticipation.

Then he stilled.

No, no, no! What now?

Luke raised his head and stared at her with something like guilt in his eyes. Glancing at the package in his hand, he said, "Shari, there's something I have to tell you. It's about the book. I—"

She giggled and kissed him, cutting off his words, glad it was only a moment's insecurity holding him back. Poor Luke, he was so passionate, and still so unsure. She was certain he was going to admit to some inadequacy that would make him feel stupid and tarnish this wonderful moment. She wanted to give him an experience so positive and blissful he'd never feel inadequate again. "You don't have to tell me anything. Too much talk spoils the mood."

He stared at her for another moment as though struggling with himself, then touched her hair. "You're right. It'll keep."

Wanting everything to go smoothly for their first time together, she took the foil package from his hand, opened it, then began to roll the condom on for him. She didn't usually do this, and was surprised at how absolutely sexy it was. He was so hot and hard that she couldn't resist squeezing and caressing him a little, until he moaned and she knew she'd better stop. As magnificent as his erection was, it wouldn't do either of them any good if he turned out to be a premature ejaculator. So she smoothed the latex over his shaft and, while she had him on his back, strad-dled him.

Keeping her gaze on his, she wrapped her fingers around him once more and rubbed the tip of his penis against herself, letting him see how much it excited her. Normally, with a new guy, she'd be much too inhibited to act like this, but with Luke she knew she had to take control, especially this very first time. She felt as proud and careful as if she were initiating a virgin. She so wanted this to be good for him.

So far, it seemed to be very good for him if his heaving chest and pumping hips were any indication. He wanted to be inside her almost as much as she wanted him there.

She made them both wait while she rubbed herself

up and down his length a few more times, increasing her own arousal to melting point, then she eased slowly onto him.

In spite of the fact that she was close to orgasm, and her body was as ready as it would ever be, she still felt the slight stretch as her body accommodated him.

He was a big man.

She took her time, and she felt his tension, sensing how badly he wanted to thrust, and that he was letting her take him at her own pace. Silently, she thanked whoever wrote the book for teaching him that all-important courtesy. Just when she thought she was so full she wouldn't be able to take any more, she found herself settled tight against Luke's hips, and knew he was in all the way. She didn't think she'd ever forget the look in his eyes. It was almost shockingly intimate, and also tender. Wanting to increase the intimacy in every way possible, she leaned forward until they were touching everywhere, then kissed him deeply.

She started to move. She started off slow, feeling the pull and slide as she grew accustomed to his size, and the building friction as she increased the pace. She rose to her knees, taking him deep, faster and faster as the wonderful, unbearable tension rose. His hands were on her breasts, her shoulders, her hips; he was tossing beneath her and she could have sworn he was straining to go deeper still. Suddenly it was all too much. She couldn't hold back.

"I'm going to… Oh… Oh, I'm going to…" Before she could complete the thought, the wave lifted her, churned her through time and space, where she only vaguely heard panting, a woman's keening cry and then the long groan of a man's satisfaction.

When she came back to herself, she was slumped against him, her head tucked under his chin. She heard his harsh breathing, and watched his chest labor. "You're not going to faint again, are you?" She was only half teasing.

He patted her shoulder and somehow ended up with her breast in his hand. She didn't think it was an accident. "I might. If I don't outright die."

12

SHARI'S CURLS TICKLED his chin where she lay tucked against him, her smooth, warm limbs tangled with his. Her breath wafted over his chest. She felt good curled up against him. Right, somehow.

"Shari," he said, knowing he couldn't go on deceiving her, not when they'd just made love, not when they were about to enact a repeat performance the second he got his lungs functioning again. "There's something I want to tell you."

"Oh, me, too." She tilted her head so she could look at him and, since he was only human and had just had some of the greatest sex of his life, he couldn't resist kissing her.

"Mmm," she said after what was supposed to be a friendly little kiss turned full-blown passionate, and he had to start over again retrieving his breath. "I want to tell you that most women really love it when a man talks to them in the bedroom." She shot him a glance. "And I don't mean talking dirty, though that can be fun." She kissed him softly. "You're really good at that. At talking."

He stared at her. She was totally getting into this intimate tutoring role. He wondered if she even knew she was using a teacher's voice on him. A startling possibility occurred to him. Was she so free and uninhibited with him because she assumed she had more experience and technique than he did? He could imagine that happening, and he loved the thought that by helping him, she was giving him all of herself. What a crazy idea.

He'd tried twice now to tell her he was the author of the damn book and both times she'd shut him up before he got a chance. Perhaps fate was at work here. There was no harm in his small deception, after all. It wasn't as if anyone was getting hurt. He was having the time of his life—and the sex of his life—and she was quite clearly enjoying her role as teacher.

And, after usually being the instigator of sex and the aggressor, Luke wasn't a man to say no when told to lie back and enjoy the ride.

He chuckled, unable to help himself. Her head bobbed up and down with his chest as laughter shook him. "What?"

"I was just thinking what an excellent teacher you are."

"It's a gift."

He rolled her onto her back so that he ended up on top of her. "You in my bed is a gift," he said. Enough already with him being the passive one. She could play teacher anytime she wanted, but right now, he felt like showing her a few moves of his own.

Her eyes widened when he made it evident to her that his cock was all perked up and ready to party. "Again?"

"You got a problem with that?" he said, grinning down at her, enjoying the sight of her curls tossed all over the pillow.

A smug female smirk met his gaze. "Oo-ooh, no," she said, wrapping her arms around his neck and pulling him down for a kiss.

He had a new condom on in record time. Luke slipped inside her at the same time he slipped his tongue into her mouth. Wet sweetness seemed to engulf him everywhere. He wanted to keep on kissing her and he wanted to watch her face as he took her over the edge. He solved his dilemma by kissing her for a while and then pulling back to watch her for a while. Now that the frantic edge of lust had abated, he could take his time and enjoy a slower ride. He watched her eyes darken and her cheeks flush, then her hair danced on his pillow as she began to toss her head. Her breathing turned to panting and was then lost in high-pitched cries.

He grabbed her hips and raised them, and she wrapped her legs tight around his waist. He wanted to wait, wanted to watch her through every stage of climax before seeking his own pleasure, but he was balanced on the knife edge of his own keen desire.

She was so close he felt her tightening around his cock, squeezing him with her inner muscles until sweat popped out on his forehead at the effort of holding himself in check. He thought one of them might burst if the pressure didn't let off soon. And then her hand snuck under him before he realized what she was doing, and she was holding his balls, squeezing them gently.

It must be instinct that had her squeezing to the same rhythm as her clenching inner muscles, but it was too much. He couldn't hold back. With a great moaning roar, he thrust deep and fast, tossing her over the edge and diving in right alongside her.

SHARI AWOKE, groggy but content, her body curved against Luke's.

"Morning," a sleepy male voice murmured, so close his breath stirred her hair, tickled the back of her neck.

"Morning," she replied, feeling not quite ready to face him. She was naked and wore no makeup. She hadn't intended to stay the night, but somewhere along the line she'd fallen asleep.

Waking together implied an intimacy she wasn't ready for in this very odd relationship.

"Coffee?" he asked on a yawn.

She raised her head and squinted at the clock, more to buy herself a bit of time than because she cared what time it was. It was Saturday. She could stay in bed all day if she wanted to. The rush of warmth that suffused her at the thought had her blinking. It was just after nine. Late for her, but then she didn't often make love far into the night.

It was rarer still for her to sleep over at a man's place. In fact, she hadn't done it since Gary and that had been more than six months ago.

Realizing she still hadn't answered Luke's question, she decided pleading a fictitious morning appointment when she was too fuzzy-headed to think of anything half believable would only feel childish. "Thanks. I'd love some."

Unlike her, Luke seemed totally unfazed about slipping out of bed naked. She was awfully glad he did as it allowed her to peek and confirm that every part of his physique looked as strong and lean and wonderful as it felt.

He scratched his chest, yawned and dug into the old oak dresser for sweats that he slipped on without any underwear. Yum.

He disappeared into the bathroom and came out a couple of minutes later with a faded navy terry-cloth robe. "Here," he said, laying it across her knees. "Borrow that if you like."

"Thanks." She waited until he'd left the room to slip the robe on and to take her turn in the bathroom. Her hair was a wreck, her face a little pale from lack of sleep, and her eyes and lips a bit swollen. *Passion-drunk.* The term went through her head and seemed to fit the image of the smugly disheveled woman in the mirror. Except this one looked passion-hungover.

She ran her tongue across her teeth and grimaced. She'd gone to sleep without brushing her teeth, something she never, ever did.

She considered her predicament. Her own toothbrush, plus spares, were in her apartment upstairs, but coffee was down here. Luke was certainly neat—neater than she was, anyway. Perhaps he had extras. Sure enough, when she clicked open the medicine cabinet, there were two unopened brushes. Delighted with her find, she brushed her teeth and with a shrug, used Luke's hairbrush.

Back in bed, she was propped on pillows, still wearing the bathrobe when he came in with the coffee and newspaper.

"Milk, no sugar, right?"

She nodded, inordinately pleased that he'd remembered from last night how she liked her coffee.

As he crawled in beside her, his own coffee in hand, splitting the newspaper and giving her half—as though they'd spent hundreds of nights together instead of just the one—she asked the question that had plagued her since she'd woken.

"Where are we in the book?"

A page rustled. "Ahead of schedule, but following along nicely."

She stared at his profile. They couldn't possibly be. "But…are you saying? I mean…last week?"

He grinned at her. "Chapter five. 'To the Brink and Back.' Get her so hot she'll be coming back for more."

"But that's crazy." She'd like to meet the author of that book. She'd give him, or her, or them such a piece of her mind. Women weren't that predictable.

"You're here, aren't you?"

So she was, but not because of some lame book. Was she? "You make it sound like a game."

He stared at her in surprise. "It is a game." He ran a finger between the crossed lapels of his robe where the swell of her breasts was revealed. "Seduction, courtship, sex—it's the greatest game of all."

"No. I don't believe that. It's not a game to me."

"Last night was chapter six."

She rolled her eyes. "Six for sex. How obvious."

"Obvious worked for me last night."

It had worked for her, too, but she wasn't admitting that. She thought for a minute. If last night was only chapter six, then… "What's in chapter seven?"

Luke turned to gaze at her for a long moment, then, throwing back the covers, got out of bed, disappeared and returned a few minutes later with the garish red book she'd seen drop onto his floor.

Crawling back into bed, he handed her the book. She flipped it open, wishing she hadn't asked. She didn't care. Besides, it was a bit embarrassing reading it in bed naked with the man who'd just become her lover.

She flicked through pages, trying to ignore the diagrams, and found it at last. She choked with laughter. "I don't believe this guy. Chapter seven. 'Lap It Up. Your Guide to Oral Satisfaction.'"

"Don't mock it till you've tried it," he told her, and licked his lips deliberately.

"Oh, stop." She shut the book with a thunk and put it on the night table, then picked up her half of the newspaper.

Reading in bed with Luke was so snug and intimate that she felt like part of an old married couple—except for the very new, very potent sexual hum in the air.

He'd given her the front news section and she peeked over his shoulder, expecting him to be buried in the sports pages, only to find him pulling out department store flyers.

"What are your plans for the day?" she asked, only increasing her feeling of old married coupledom.

"I have to go shopping for a wedding present for my dad."

"Your father's getting married for a second time?"

He snorted. "The fifth time. We've got bets on who ends up with the high score, him or Liz Taylor."

"Wow. That's a lot of weddings. Does he have some sort of…um, issue?"

"He's a determined optimist, I guess."

From the cynicism in Luke's voice, he didn't seem to share the trait.

"What a coincidence. So am I."

"A determined optimist?"

She chuckled. "Yes. I guess I am. But I meant I'm going wedding present shopping today, too. For B.J.'s wedding."

He glanced up from the JC Penney flyer. "Want to go together?"

"Your father's been married four times?" She still couldn't get past this rather startling fact.

"Yep." You could pack a lot of emotion into one "yep" but Luke didn't bother to do it. He sounded fine with his dad's many marriages. Hmm.

"Which union produced you?"

He glanced at her with a glimmer of humor. "You might say I started the whole train rolling. I was the reason for the first marriage."

"You mean, your mother was…" She petered out, trying to find a sensitive way to ask.

"Knocked up with me, yeah."

"Oh." She didn't know what else to say.

"You'd think he'd have learned a lesson about sloppy birth control, but—" Luke shook his head sharply and his annoyance was clear. Where he hadn't seemed to mind about the four wives, the unplanned pregnancies had him narrowing his lips.

"Some men aren't cut out for marriage," he said. "My dad should have steered clear of the altar."

"I'm sorry, Luke," she said, wishing there was a way to help him overcome his cynicism about relationships that would be as quick and effective as the book that had launched him on the path to being an outstanding lover.

"My mom always tells me I'm like my dad." He

tossed the papers aside and leaned back, and she heard both pride and defensiveness in his tone.

"Are you?" she asked softly, sensing that what he believed might be nothing like the truth.

He snorted. "I'm not going to marry a string of nice women, if that's what you mean. And I don't care what a woman tells me about any birth control she's on, I always use a condom. Always."

"That's sensible, anyway, in this day and age," she said, feeling a creeping sadness for Luke.

"How about your mother? Did she marry again?" she asked delicately.

"You don't know my mother. Being the betrayed first wife is pretty much a vocation with her."

"Ouch."

"Yeah. It's too nice a day to go into my dysfunctional family. All four of them."

"Surely you only grew up in one family."

"Well, theoretically, but Dad liked the fantasy of one big happy family, so every summer we'd get together at a cabin he owns. All the kids together.

"Mum had three kids, and two of the other wives had two each. Of course the last few are a lot younger." He shrugged. "Most of us still turn up every summer."

"It must be something," she said, trying to picture seven assorted half brothers and sisters getting together every year.

"You can see it if you like," he said, focusing fiercely on his coffee mug. "Dad's getting married out there the week after your friend's wedding. You'll meet most of the sibs."

He was inviting her to his father's wedding. Wow.

That felt almost serious. She wasn't sure, after one night with him, that she wanted to commit to being his girlfriend, with all that that implied. And yet, why not? Stalling for time, she said, "You must all get on with one another."

"Mostly. They're a decent bunch, and it's not the kids' fault Dad can't keep his pants zipped."

"Is the next Mrs. Lawson…" She fluttered her hand in front of her belly.

"Pregnant? Oh, no. We all chipped in and bought Dad a vasectomy for his fiftieth birthday. We didn't think another Lawson was going to do the world any favors."

"Your dad didn't mind?"

"Hell, no. I think he was relieved." He toyed with her hair, skimming his fingers behind her ear. "So will you?"

She drained the last of her coffee. "Go with you to your father's wedding?"

He sent her a crafty glance. "I'm going to the boy-friend stealer's wedding. It's a fair trade."

She elbowed him sharply in the ribs. "Excuse me, but did I or did I not see you through not only four chapters of this book of yours, but all the way to chapter six?"

His eyes weren't sleepy now, they were dancing with wicked humor. "You did. How about a side deal?"

Her eyes narrowed. "What might that be?"

He had her on her back, his hand sliding beneath the lapel of his robe to find her breast so fast she didn't have time for more than a startled squeak.

Luckily her coffee mug was empty, for it fell from her shocked fingers and rolled to the floor.

"Chapter seven."

When she tried to squirm out of his grip she merely increased the friction of his hand on her breast, which made her giggle and turned her on simultaneously. "Stop!" she cried. "Stop! You're tickling me."

"I don't think I'm tickling you. I think I'm exciting you."

She was so busy wriggling and giggling that she didn't even notice he'd untied the belt and opened her robe until she felt his lips close over her breast, his tongue teasing her nipple. "Lap it up," he said, repeating the chapter title.

Before she knew it, her laughter turned to panting and arousal spiraled through her belly.

"No, no," she panted. "No sex before breakfast."

He raised his head to grin at her. "Eat fast. Then I'm going to eat you." He kissed her lightly on the lips. "Slowly."

A low moan rose in her throat, and she swallowed it down ruthlessly. She was sliding far too deep into Luke's messy life. And frankly, he was sliding far too deep into her body. She needed some space to sort things out.

His chapter seven threat hung in the air as they got out of bed and padded to the kitchen with their coffee mugs.

"Let's see what there is," he said as he opened the fridge. "Aha, dessert…" He turned and winked at her. "We never did get ours last night."

"Dessert. For breakfast." She shook her head at

him in mock rebuke as she helped herself to a clean
cup from the cupboard. "What is it?"

"Blueberry pie."

"Seems a shame to waste it."

"That's what I was thinking." She refilled their
mugs, and he dished up two very generous slices of
pie. He raised his brows at her and grinned wickedly.
"Ice cream?"

Refusing such a challenge would be cowardly.
"Why not?" she replied, and bit her tongue on the
automatic, *but not too much for me.*

As she ate last night's dessert, she decided that
blueberry pie and ice cream was a pretty good breakfast once in a while. Besides, since she was in fact
eating yesterday's calories, it hardly counted.

"Are your father and his, um, fiancée registered
anywhere?"

"You mean, like the kennel club?"

"That's very disrespectful," she said, trying not to
giggle. "No, I meant bridal registry for gifts."

"I don't think he needs a fifth set of china and
flatware."

"Well, no, but the bride might."

Having cleaned his plate, he licked his spoon clean.
She couldn't watch his tongue sweep the last vestiges
of creamy ice cream off the silver spoon and not think
of chapter seven. And she couldn't think of chapter
seven and not tremble deep inside.

"I can see I'm going to have to explain my wedding present philosophy to you."

"This I have to hear." She spooned up the last
berry smothered in half-melted ice cream and found
she was looking forward to Luke's philosophy. The

man never ceased to surprise her with his silliness. She was so routine-oriented and predictable, she wondered if a little silliness was in fact good for her.

She suspected it was.

"You can't stop people getting married. But let's face it, you know when you go to a wedding there's at least a fifty percent chance it won't last. In my dad's case, a hundred percent. As a wedding guest, and a friend of at least one of the parties getting married, I feel it's my duty to save them some grief down the road. I'm determined not to give them something that will end up fought over in the divorce. My presents have a short shelf life."

"Really, this is fascinating." It was also a pretty cynical attitude, but given his family situation, she supposed it was understandable. "How short a life span?"

"Now that's the scientific part." His eyes twinkled as he leaned forward, but there was seriousness there, as well. "I try to make an educated guess on how much time they've got. The extreme would be a bottle of champagne and two glasses, with the card telling them to smash the glasses after drinking—for good luck."

"So you'd only buy crystal if it was going to be smashed."

"Absolutely."

"And you'd never buy china."

"Nope, it's got permanence written all over it. Same with flatware."

"How about linens?"

"Depends. Towels are good. You need new towels

every couple of years. Fancy tablecloths and things? Forget it. It's like china.''

"Well, my philosophy is to assume every couple whose wedding I attend will see their golden anniversary. B.J.'s registered at Percy and Fitz, and I also need to look for an outfit for the wedding."

"No problem. I'll carry your bags."

The idea of having her own personal shopping sherpa was undeniably appealing. "You don't mind?"

"We can help each other."

"Okay. I have to shower first and change my clothes. How about I come down and get you in about half an hour?"

"Perfect."

He waved her off when she tried to clear the table, so she ran back into the bedroom and changed into her frumpy clothes from yesterday. She emerged to find him wiping down the kitchen counter.

She picked up her purse by the couch and then wasn't sure about whether to kiss him goodbye or not. "Well, thanks for dinner," she said, and started for the door. She'd made her intentions clear; she was leaving. What he did with that information was up to him.

What he did was dump the cloth in the sink and speed to her side.

She wasn't sure the kiss could be classified as a goodbye-and-thanks-for-dinner kiss. It wasn't the sort of kiss you'd lay on your grandmother, for instance, or a casual friend.

She moaned as she clasped him tighter, thrusting

her fingers into his messy hair and causing further disarray.

The kiss turned steamier, and suddenly she found herself backed against Luke's door, his body hard and flush against hers. She was melting faster than ice cream over warmed blueberry pie.

"Oh, that feels good." She broke contact with his mouth long enough to gasp, "I have to shower."

Right. Shower.

"You are obsessed with personal hygiene," he growled, but with a final nibbling trail down her throat that had her reconsidering her obsession, he let her go.

"See you in half an hour."

13

LEXINGTON GALLERIA was an upmarket shopping center with three levels, wrought-iron railings and a tuxedoed pianist tinkling away on a grand piano on the third floor. The most expensive floor. The one to which Shari dragged Luke.

"Figures this is where she'd have bridal registry."

"Percy and Fitz," Luke read the store name aloud. "Should be Pricey and Pretentious."

"Shh." She motioned him to pipe down, and they entered the hallowed marble hallways with its snooty staff and fingerprint-free glass cases.

A woman who could have passed for Queen Elizabeth approached them. "May I help you?"

Determined to be gracious at the wedding and not by word or deed to let B.J. and Randy think she so much as remembered having her heart ripped out and spat on, Shari explained to the woman why they were there, and then studied the list she produced of household items the couple wanted.

Discarding things like "Dishwasher, Bosch" as too expensive and any knives as possibly sending messages of suppressed violent feelings, she was still left with plenty of gift choices.

While Luke studied martini glasses carefully—searching for the most breakable, she was certain—

she hovered indecisively between a place setting of china and a set of sterling napkin rings. She preferred the napkin rings, but, unless B.J. had changed, she'd be judging her presents by the size of the box they arrived in.

When Luke wandered by while she was in mid-dither, the Queen Elizabeth salesclerk said, "Perhaps your husband might have an opinion?"

At the same moment she said, "Oh, we're not—" Luke said, "We're just—"

She stared at him as his words petered out and she wondered what the end of that sentence was. What were they, exactly? And how did he think of them now that they'd spent the night together?

Not that she had any complaints about last night— far, far from it—she'd sensed a certain holding back and assumed his slight hesitance was based on lack of experience or whatever disastrous fumbles had previously occurred in his sex life. Still, she hoped he didn't get too serious too fast.

A quick, hot flash of panic seared her belly; perhaps shopping for wedding presents the morning after they'd first slept together wasn't the brightest idea.

"The place setting," she decided. "And I'd like it gift-wrapped and delivered."

"Of course. Have you your own card or would you care to choose from our selection?"

Naturally, Shari hadn't thought to bring along a wedding card, so she grabbed one with a bland verse and hearts and flowers on the cover, dug a pen out of her bag and signed it, "Love, Shari and Luke." She may not want Luke thinking they were a couple, but she definitely wanted B.J. thinking it.

Luke loitered a bit over the martini glasses, which were so thin she felt they'd break if she looked at them too closely. But eventually he decided to pass and to see what else they could find.

They wandered out of Percy and Fitz and Shari had the pleasant feeling of having discharged one of her obligations. The outfit was next, and it was by far the bigger job. She really wasn't certain she wanted Luke around, though, while she tried on clothes. If he was anything like her brother, Luke's shopping tolerance wouldn't get him past the first dress, which, as every woman knew, and no man seemed to understand, never fit.

"Do you want to look for something else for your father's wedding?" she asked brightly.

He turned to gaze down at her, sleepy green eyes wrinkling at the corners. "You wouldn't be trying to get out of me seeing you in a whole lot of slinky, strapless things would you?"

Absobloodylutely. But she wasn't going to tell him that. "No. I don't want to hog your Saturday, that's all."

"No problem. I can shop anytime. You've only got the weekends, right?"

"Well, yes, but we could split up…?"

With an arm around her shoulders he pulled her close, put his mouth to her ear and spoke softly. "Not before chapter seven."

How did he do this to her? She immediately felt as shivery as a virgin bride contemplating her wedding night.

Shari had a pretty good idea what was in chapter seven, but somehow he made it sound as if they'd been visiting some exotic foreign land. Heat bubbled through her veins as it occurred to her that he might be a bit of a novice at oral sex and need guidance. Once more she'd be Shari, personal guide to all things sexual.

She could teach him to please her; she could give him pleasure he may never have experienced before. She had to admit, when Luke had gone looking for a teacher, he could have done a lot worse.

Since they happened to be passing a ritzy boutique, she decided to test his mettle as a shopping companion and tugged him through the entrance. He followed her obediently from rack to rack, letting her flip rapidly through outfits, looking for exactly the right thing. She pulled out a pale green sheath dress with matching jacket that begged for a hat and pumps. A possibility. She handed it off to the hovering saleswoman who spirited it away to the discreet dressing cubicles.

There was a lavender pantsuit that appealed to her, but since it was an evening reception with dancing, that seemed too casual. Finally she ended up with a pale yellow dress with a fitted bodice and full skirt, and the green two-piece.

Luke settled into an armchair while she disappeared into the change room. She'd put on strappy high heels deliberately, knowing she'd be trying on things for the wedding. She also wore pretty lingerie, but if she was honest with herself, that was mostly for later. All this finery she'd hid under a stretchy purple cotton dress that pulled on and off with the ease of a T-shirt. She was doing her best to make this shopping excursion as effortless as possible.

The green two-piece fit nicely. With the jacket it was perfect for the wedding ceremony; she could slip it off when the dancing started. She stepped outside and modeled it for Luke, rather enjoying the way his gaze took a long, lazy tour of her body in the dress.

"Take off the jacket," he said. Did he have any idea what that intimate tone did to her? Probably, if he was looking in the direction of her chest, he did. If he said "Take off your dress," in that same sexy drawl, she probably would. Right in front of the sales associates and the other customers.

He didn't, though, only motioning her to turn around, which she did, hoping the dress didn't pull at the hips.

"What do you think?" she asked him, when he'd finished scrutinizing.

"I'm ready for the next choice. Don't want to make any snap decisions."

She shook her head at him and slipped back into the dressing room. Her own feeling was that it wasn't bad as first dresses went, but it hadn't wowed her, either. However, superstitiously she believed a good first dress could be a sign that success was just around the corner.

Maybe the yellow…

She stepped into it, feeling like a sixties prom queen. The full skirt was fun, the bodice fit perfectly. Out she stepped to stand in front of Luke.

There was something almost erotic about posing and spinning while a man, relaxing in an armchair, stared at you. It felt as though she were being judged or auditioned for something. And the way Luke's gaze traveled over her, there was no doubt that wedding finery wasn't on his mind. He licked his lips as he looked at her, and the blatant challenge in his eyes made her heart jump. If he'd whispered, ''Chapter seven,'' he couldn't have put her mind more firmly in tune with the promised activities he'd outlined for later.

''Well?'' she asked after she'd spun for him again. ''What do you think?''

He gave the thumbs-down.

''Why not?'' She couldn't help but wonder. The dress might not be the most fabulous thing she'd ever seen in her life, but it fit and was perfect for a wedding. He couldn't know she'd sneaked a peek at the price tag and almost fainted. This was a great dress. Of course, she planned to look some more, but so far she thought she had a real contender.

''Too dull for you.''

''Dull? What do you mean?''

He shot a glance at the hovering saleswoman, who was busy giving him the evil eye. ''I'll take you for lunch and we'll discuss it.''

''Don't you ever think about anything but food?'' she asked him when she'd changed back into her own clothes and they'd left the store.

''Sure. When I finish eating. Then I don't think about food until I'm hungry again.''

She let him drag her right out of the shopping center to a deli-café across the street. She ordered a salad and he ordered a clubhouse with french fries.

''What did you mean, that dress was dull?''

He sipped iced tea, as though trying to find the right words. ''I've never met this B.J., but based on all that uptight flowery stuff she wanted for wedding presents, I'd say those dresses would be perfect for her. But they're not you. You wear bright colors and your clothes have...I don't know, personality.''

Shari blinked at him. "It's just a dress."

"Is it?" He gazed at her across the table, and she felt he was seeing more than she wanted him to see. "I have three sisters, and I swear they used to dress with some kind of code book in hand. Wear black on fat days, stripes one way to make your boobs look bigger, stripes the other way to make you look taller, and they had a whole other wardrobe for church."

"Of course we wear clothes to flatter us. What's wrong with that?"

"Nothing. Women also send messages with clothes." He glanced at her, with that telltale eye-crinkling. "Like wearing purple means you want to get laid."

She glanced at her bright purple dress and choked on a laugh. "Does not."

He leaned closer. "I bet if I slipped my hand under that dress right now, I'd find you're wet for me."

All the air seemed to be squeezing out of her lungs. Five seconds ago, he'd have been dreaming, but all he had to do was look at her in that certain way, and the very idea of him touching her intimately had her squirming on the vinyl bench.

He didn't have to know that, however, and she wasn't going anywhere until she had a dress for the wedding. "I dressed like this so it would be easy to try on clothes."

"Can't blame a guy for trying." He shrugged. "I just don't think those dresses are you, that's all."

Could he possibly be right? Was she so caught up

in proving to B.J. and the rest of them that she'd made out fine in life, thank you very much, that she was choosing clothes that reflected success on their terms rather than her own?

She chomped spinach leaves with fury. Damn. She hated admitting, even to herself, that Luke was right. But, of course, he was.

The diet, the fitness program, the date, the dress.

She groaned and reached over to snag a french fry off Luke's plate. "That yellow dress was the price of a month's rent."

He whistled softly and pushed his plate closer so she could help herself.

In the end, they went to one of her favorite street-front boutiques. Luke walked in, took a look at the mannequin posed near the store entrance, and said, "That one."

It was her signature purple, in some kind of a brushed-silk fabric that was gorgeous to the touch. It had a tight-fitting bodice, spaghetti straps and a skirt that just begged to twirl on the dance floor. She tried it on and her eyes lit up in the change-room mirror. It was her. It showed her figure off to perfection— including the flat stomach it had taken several thousand sit-ups to produce.

This place didn't boast armchairs for the gentleman escorts, so Luke was standing outside when she emerged, and it was clear he liked what he saw. He twirled his finger the way a dog trainer would to a poodle, and she obligingly turned around for him. "Yep," he said. "That's the one."

"It's kind of...not revealing exactly, but...breezy for the wedding ceremony."

"I've got just the thing," said the salesclerk, Jan, as in "Hi, my name is Jan, if there's *anything* you need, give me a shout." You'd think she was planning to sell Luke dresses the way she hung by his side, Shari thought sourly.

But when the young woman returned with a silky crocheted shawl patterned in the same shade of violet with yellow, red and white accents, Shari knew she'd found her outfit.

She tried on a few more just because she felt she should, but it was the purple dress with which she'd fallen in love.

"Thank you," she said to Luke, grabbing him on the sidewalk and impulsively kissing him, holding her bags tight in her hands.

"I had fun," he said. "I don't get out much."

She'd laugh, assuming it was a joke, except she had a pretty good idea that it was true. He worked so many hours in his apartment alone he probably needed to get out among people more often. "You must be looking forward to Tuesday, then. When you speak to my class."

"Not half as much as I'm looking forward to getting you home and naked for—"

"Yeah, yeah, I know. Chapter seven." She was deliberately casual, but she had to admit his constant references to the next chapter in his how-to book were starting to arouse her. Most men she knew would be mortified even to admit to owning a sex manual, but Luke seemed to have decided, once she was in on his little secret, to treat each chapter like a new world waiting to be discovered. He made sex seem fresh and exciting.

"Do you have any more shopping to do?" he asked. "Or do you want to go straight home?"

Sure, she needed shoes and a new handbag and some sheer hose to go with her new dress. At the moment, though, there was only one item on her agenda.

Chapter seven.

"Let's go home," she said.

They didn't talk much on the way home. She felt the mounting anticipation of what they were about to do, and she couldn't wait. She reminded herself that he'd be a bit inept, but that was okay. In fact, it was kind of sweet. Besides, new lovers always needed to learn each other's bodies. If more men had asked her for help and guidance, she'd have had more winners in her sex life.

With Luke, she wasn't afraid to take the initiative and to show him how to please her. He'd asked her for guidance, but in truth she was doing this for herself as well as for him. She enjoyed her role as intimate teacher more than she'd dreamed. Who'd have believed helping a man become a terrific lover would be such a turn-on?

Oh, but it was. She was having trouble sitting still on the black leather upholstery. She wanted to wiggle. She wanted to grope. Frankly, she wanted to go down on him right here in a speeding vehicle in the middle of the highway. Which struck her as the fastest trip to the morgue, so she kept herself in check. But it wasn't easy, the heat building inside her body was becoming uncomfortable.

She glanced at Luke and his jaw was fiercely set. In fact, she felt tension coming off him in waves. Her gaze dropped to his lap and, as she suspected, he was harder than the stick shift. She turned away to hide her grin. He was as turned on as she was.

Well, maybe she couldn't physically grope him in the car, but she could have a little fun, couldn't she?

"What does it say in chapter seven?" Her voice came out sultry and teasing, and she noticed that he swallowed hard before replying.

"It says that a man can give a woman more pleasure with his tongue than any other part of his body." He sounded a little put out by that and she imagined he was as penis-centered as every other guy in the universe.

She hid her smile. "Well, I never thought of it like that, although I suppose it's true. The tongue is very flexible and comes with its own lubrication. But I like the, um, whole package."

"Well, that's a relief. Let's see, what else does it say in chapter seven?" He thought for a moment while traffic hummed outside. Neither of them had put on any music, so it was quiet inside the car but for the purr of the engine.

All of a sudden she wished she hadn't brought up the subject. Did she really want to know what it said in chapter seven? What if it advocated she do things to Luke she'd never heard of before? She was a reasonably confident woman, comfortable with her own sexuality, but she wasn't on intimate terms with the *Kama Sutra*. There were probably dozens, hundreds of sex tricks she didn't know.

"It says that asking your partner what they like is the best technique there is."

She nodded. Perhaps the guy who wrote that lame book wasn't as much of a moron as she'd assumed.

"So what do you like, Shari? Do you like a firm, back and forth stroke of a man's tongue over your clit or a lighter, licking motion?"

"I, um…" Damn it, she'd planned to torture him, how dare he turn the tables and torture her? His words conjured images in her head of his mouth doing those things to her until she was burning.

Still, she had to remember he wasn't doing this to torture her. He really didn't know. She had to be patient. She cleared her throat and tried to think of this as a learning moment. "I like both. I, uh, like a lighter touch to start with, and then when I'm more…excited, a stronger stroke works for me." Oh, God, this was embarrassing. Why hadn't she kept her big mouth shut? She knew she was blushing, which just exacerbated her discomfort.

He nodded, and she had the feeling that if his hands weren't currently occupied with driving he'd be taking notes! "What about your G-spot?" he asked in an earnest-student tone. "Do you like to have it massaged while a man licks you?"

Oh, oh, oh. It felt as if he were massaging it now. His words, and the images they evoked, made her so ultrasensitive that even the slight vibration of the car engine through her seat was driving her close to the edge. It was a good thing Luke was too clueless to have any idea what he was doing to her, or she'd have to hurt him.

"I—I like it fine. It can sometimes take a little time to find the G-spot, but I'll let you know when you get warm.'' She fanned her face with her hand. ''Speaking of warm, do you mind if I open the window?''

''Sure,'' he said, and his voice quivered. If it were any other man she'd suspect he was trying not to laugh, but with Luke it might just be nerves.

She pushed the button to lower the window and let the spring air wash over her heated face.

''There's a diagram in the book that shows a man taking the entire clitoris inside his mouth. I wasn't sure whether he'd suck it like a peppermint, say, or lick it like the tip of an ice-cream cone. What do you think you'd prefer?''

''Please, we have to change the subject now,'' she gasped, feeling at any moment she was going to give the passengers in the Greyhound chugging along beside them a view of her in the throes of orgasm.

''Okay, sure.'' He shot her a quick glance before turning his attention back to the road. It was only for a fleeting second, but she could have sworn he was holding back a grin.

Her eyes narrowed. ''Did you, by any chance, do that on purpose?''

''Do what?''

Shari was as cute when she was suspicious as she was when she was explaining her response to oral sex as though it were an algebra equation she was trying to help him understand.

She was so aroused from their little verbal lesson he could feel the heat coming off her body. Luke was sorely tempted to take a hand off the steering wheel, shove it up her skirt and put her out of her misery. But then, he was suffering as badly.

If he hadn't been following his book so carefully,

he'd have gone down on her last night. He'd ached to do it. Having touched her there, and thrust inside her, he'd longed to take her with his mouth, to taste her pleasure.

He found, however, that having made himself wait to taste her, he'd only become more eager for the opportunity. And, thanks to the way he'd been reminding her all day of exactly what they were going to do, his agenda was as clear as the view of her glorious body when he got her naked and spread out on his bed.

He shifted uncomfortably, resisting the urge to floor it. Every particle of his being burned with need. He couldn't play games anymore. "I need you. Now. If I don't get my tongue on you I'm going to lose it."

Her answer was a strangled moan.

They were both panting when he pulled into his parking stall on a squeal of brakes. They had their respective doors open faster than a pair of cops at a crime scene.

He grabbed her hand and ran. Not the elevator, too slow. He yanked open the heavy metal door to the stairs and they sprinted up to the second floor, ran down the hall, his keys jangling in his hand. It took him two tries to jab the key into the lock and then, finally, they were inside his apartment.

"My bags," she cried in a stunned voice, even as he grabbed for her.

"Automatic locks. Leave them."

He took her grunted reply as a yes, then pulled her to him and devoured her mouth.

14

IT WAS A GOOD THING she already thought he was a clumsy oaf, for he was beyond finesse, beyond conscious thought, driven only by need.

For the second time in their short relationship, he hoisted her into his arms and for the second time she shivered in reaction. He strode to his bedroom, kicked the door open and deposited her on her back on the bed.

He kneeled over her, enjoying her rapid breathing, dazed eyes and swollen lips. "Time for chapter seven."

She moaned and he had a feeling *chapter seven* would forever be part of their vocabulary. A personal lovers' code. The word *forever* flashed and danced across his brain before he banished it and prepared to enjoy one very hot woman.

She was fully dressed, but his urgency was too great to mess around with undressing her. For now, he only needed one part of her naked. He hiked up her skirt in one jerk, flipping it right up over her hips.

Her eyes darkened and she raised her hands over her head as though to reach for something to anchor her. *Not going to work.*

He nudged her legs apart and dropped his gaze,

only to find himself groaning. "Oh, Shari. What have you done?"

"Surprise." The word seemed a struggle for her. Her hips were starting to twitch with the wanting, but he had to pause for a moment and enjoy the sight of old-fashioned stockings that stopped at midthigh. Her lacy garter belt and panties were bright, in-your-face purple. He touched the creamy skin of her upper thighs and her breath hitched. No. He couldn't go slowly. He wanted to, but he couldn't. Maybe later. For now he had to see her, touch her, taste her.

His hands shook as he slipped off the panties. If she noticed she'd put it down to nerves, when in fact it was desire, stronger than any he'd ever experienced, that rocked him.

He trailed her silk panties down her legs and, to please himself, let them hang from one of her strappy high heels. He liked the picture she made, he definitely liked it. Her eyes were closed and she was in someplace all her own.

He smiled as he moved to kneel between her thighs. Knowing he'd teased them both enough, he parted her, found her moist and pink, her obvious arousal sending the need to have her straight to his groin. He was never selfish with women, but this one had him almost mindless with the most basic urge to take and mate.

But the urge to pleasure her was just as strong.

Remembering what she'd told him, even though he'd only asked to tease, he followed her instructions, beginning with a light delicate touch that had her opening for him like a bud to sunshine, exposing her glossy pink clit. He gave it a light flicking with his tongue and felt it quiver and harden.

Even the most ignorant novice could tell this lady was close to exploding. Deciding he'd have lots of time to toy with her later, he changed to firmer sweeping tongue strokes and pretty much had to hold her hips in both hands to keep her earthbound. She progressed rapidly from panting to moaning. Everything beneath his tongue was getting slicker and plumper, and then, since he was holding her hips in place, her upper body rose as he felt the shudders of climax rock her.

Once, she rose to half sitting and fell back. Twice, and then she sighed delightfully.

He took a couple of minutes to kiss her thighs and stroke any part of her he could reach, while she slowly floated back to earth. He didn't let her get her feet on the ground, though, before going back for dessert.

She chuckled and touched her hand to his head as he resumed the soft licking he'd started her with. "No. I couldn't. Not so soon."

In answer, he slipped a finger inside her where the last contractions from her orgasm clasped him like tiny hugs. He pushed a second finger inside, and she sighed and shifted. He probed gently until he found the dense mound of her G-spot and began to massage it lightly.

She gasped. *Not ready to go again, huh?* He grinned against her soft, moist flesh, and then put his tongue to her. He avoided the clit since it was still probably too sensitive, but he explored all her secret folds and crevices, working with a light touch here, a firmer one there, and gauged her response from her sighs and moans and the way her body once more bloomed for him.

All the while, he kept massaging the magic spot inside her.

"Oh, that feels so good," she cried when he returned to her clit, which was once again blushing in eagerness.

He'd only been toying with her about taking her clit right into his mouth, but it seemed like a pretty good idea.

He tried it.

She liked it.

In fact, she liked it so much she screamed, and he had the pleasure of feeling her pleasure burst inside his mouth like summer-sweet fruit. He stayed with her through the aftershocks and brought her gently back to earth once more.

He was only human, and the seat of his own pleasure had been screaming for attention long enough. Rising, he began to strip off his clothes, wanting to be inside her to catch the last of her contractions.

He was naked in seconds, fumbling for his night table, when she stopped him.

"My turn," she said.

With her heavy-lidded eyes, and her hair tangled from thrashing on the pillow, she looked like a well-loved Gypsy.

That wasn't an offer he was about to turn down. But he'd held himself back so long, he was worried he might embarrass himself. "I'm not sure how long I'll last," he told her honestly, not wanting the party to end the minute she invited him in the door.

She smiled and pushed him down on the bed. Then she kicked aside the panties that were still hanging from her shoe, rose to stand beside the bed and, slowly and erotically, pulled her dress over her head.

Once again he groaned. Of course the panties and garter belt had a matching brassiere, and of course it made him salivate to see her generous breasts barely contained in the lacy purple, the dusky nipples playing peekaboo through the fabric. "They should sell blood-pressure medication along with those things." He moaned, watching her. She didn't remove the shoes, or the stockings and garter belt, but she did, after an agonizing minute, slip off the bra.

Luke loved breasts. All breasts. Large ones, small ones, black ones, white ones, Asian ones; he loved the bounce and curve and the personality of every pair. But he'd never seen breasts that he loved as much as these. He could have sworn they flirted with him. Bouncing jauntily as she knelt beside him on the bed, brushing against him.

If he'd ever been this hard, he didn't remember the time. He was literally quivering to have that beautiful, warm, full-lipped mouth on him.

She shot him a teasing glance and wrapped her small, capable hand around the base of his penis. He was close to weeping.

"Now. Do you like light gentle licks? Or do you prefer a long, stronger stroke?"

Damn it, she was on to him. He never should have teased her in the car. "Anything," he begged. "I'll take anything."

She chuckled and, since she was obviously a woman of compassion, didn't tease him any longer.

She simply opened her mouth and sucked him inside where it was warm and wet and her tongue danced on his flesh. Sweat broke out on his brow as he fought the urge to explode. His blood was thundering in his ears, his breath sounding like that of a winded marathon runner.

There was only one way he could prevent imminent humiliation. Grabbing her shoulders when she came up for air, he flipped her onto her back and covered her body with his own. While he kissed that beautiful mouth that gave him so much pleasure, he reached for a condom.

Then he entered her in one swift, hard thrust. Now he let his inner caveman out. The poor guy deserved a break. His loving wasn't pretty, or suave; he pumped into her with all the pent-up agony and frustration of the wait, and with all the suppressed desire in him.

Instead of being turned off by his crude rutting, she seemed to get into the spirit of the thing, hooking her legs around his hips and joining in the frenzied mating with enthusiasm. They roared like a pair of jungle lions as climax shook them; she stuffed the handiest thing into her mouth to quell her cries. Unfortunately, that something was his shoulder. Even as he came in a hot rush, he was conscious of the sharp pain of her teeth biting into him.

Afterward, they collapsed, sweating and exhausted, into sleep.

It was dark when he awoke. And he was hungry.

Shari slept on beside him, her hair in sexy tangles from their wild lovemaking. God, she was gorgeous. He decided to let her sleep while he rustled up some food, but a trip to the fridge informed him there wasn't much in there.

His stomach growled as he dug out peanut butter and a loaf of bread.

"What time is it?" a sleepy voice asked.

She stood there, heavy-eyed, her hair a beautiful mess, his robe hanging to her ankles, and he wanted her again. He couldn't get enough of her. He was acting as though he were the eager novice she believed him to be; a guy who'd only just discovered sex and was suddenly obsessed. Which was exactly how he felt.

Dropping his gaze to his watch, he said, "Almost six."

"Is that dinner?"

He spread peanut butter onto bread in a generous swipe. "Nope. Before-dinner snack. I'm starving."

"You're always hungry."

He grinned at her. "I'm a man of healthy appetites." He sank his teeth into his peanut butter sandwich, but he let his gaze rove her body deliberately, letting her know he was only fueling up until it was time to indulge his favorite appetite.

One eyebrow arched as she stared back at him.

"Want one?" He gestured to the jar and the bread.

"No, thank you. Do you want to come up to my place for dinner? I've got some casseroles in the freezer."

"I want to come up to your place. Dinner's a good start."

She chuckled and disappeared into the bedroom.

He polished off his sandwich and then followed her.

She'd pulled her dress back on, but it was wrinkled. He liked the fact than anyone she would pass in the hall was going to know damn well what she'd been doing with her Saturday afternoon.

"I love how organized you are," he said. Shari was the kind of woman who had casseroles in the freezer. Stuff like that always impressed him.

He dragged on jeans and a shirt and they headed up to her place, where he tried to forget the fact that the last time he'd been here he'd lost consciousness.

She went straight to the freezer, so she must be as hungry as he was. "Vegetarian chili? Potato-and-cheese soup? Or...hmm, the label fell off. Mystery casserole?"

As though he did it every night, he walked to the cutlery drawer and took out knives and forks. "Let's have mystery casserole. I feel adventurous." He even remembered where she kept the placemats and napkins.

"I've got wine and beer in the fridge, if you like," she said, taking the foil cover off the dish and inspecting it. With a shrug she stuck it into the microwave.

He opened the small freezer above her fridge just to have another look at the neatly stacked casserole dishes. "This is amazing."

She chuckled. "It's mostly survival. I'm usually too tired to cook when I get home from work, and who wants to make a full meal for one person? So, since I love to cook, I make a stew, or soup or pasta and freeze it into smaller portions." She scratched her nose. "It sounds kind of 'lonely single woman,' I guess, but it works for me."

"No." He shut the freezer door and turned to stare at her. "It's terrific. I eat way too much take-out because I'm lazy. Well, I also go out a lot because I work alone and live alone. There are days my larynx could fall out while I'm brushing my teeth and I'd never notice. Sometimes I never talk to anyone all day."

"That sounds like heaven. I'm talking all day—" she grinned "—or yelling for order or listening to hundreds of high school kids. You'll find out on Tuesday. Your larynx may fall out from overuse."

"I'm looking forward to it." And amazingly, he was. He was curious to see Shari in her work environment. He had a feeling she'd be a dedicated teacher. He bet she was also the unknowing recipient of a few male teenage fantasies.

She also probably had a busy social life and he was horning in on it. "It's Saturday night. I'm not keeping you from something, am I?"

"No, I—" She gasped and slapped a hand across her open mouth. "Oh, I forgot. I do have plans. It's the going-away party for one of the teachers. I can't believe I almost forgot." She blushed adorably when she glanced his way. "I've had my mind on other things. Chapter seven is a personal favorite."

"No problem," he said, not happy about the tug of disappointment in his belly. He was Mr. Casual. He shouldn't care that Shari already had plans for tonight. But he did care. He hadn't spent nearly enough time naked with her, or enough time just talking. "I'll head out and find a burger or something."

"No, don't do that. We've got time for dinner. The going-away party is at one of the teachers' houses.

We were all invited to bring someone if we wanted. You're welcome to come with me.''

Usually, he avoided other people's work things like the plague, but a Saturday night without Shari didn't hold a lot of appeal.

"Okay, I'll come with you, if you're sure."

"I'm sure." She eased closer and placed her lips against his neck.

"There are a few more diagrams I'd like to explore in chapter seven."

That Lance Flagstaff had created a monster.

Luke would love to buy the guy a beer.

If he wasn't already living inside Lance's skin.

Since when had his life turned into this weird combination of fiction and fantasy?

He was going to have to admit to Shari that he'd written *Sex for TMs*. He knew that. But she was having so much fun tutoring him and he was having as much fun letting her that he wasn't quite ready to let the real world intrude. An annoying little voice inside him whispered that he was in trouble here. Shari was showing up in his idle dreams about the future, and more and more he was seeing her in his fictitious psychiatrist—the one who would be pivotal in saving or damning his tortured hero. Once again, he wondered about the fine line between fantasy and reality.

As his father's son, he had to accept that he wasn't the right man for Shari with her romantic heart, her china patterns and golden wedding anniversary dreams. He'd have to come clean soon.

But not quite yet.

15

WHAT HAD URGED HER to invite Luke? Shari wondered as she finished dressing. After discovering the mystery casserole was beef stroganoff and quite tasty if she did say so herself, Luke had gone to his place to shower and change, and she was doing the same in her apartment.

If she hadn't already promised to go to the goodbye party for Cliff Masters, she'd be awfully tempted to stay home. Luke was a comfortable man to be with as well as an exciting one. She could talk to him some more about his novel, maybe con a few more chapters out of him. They'd have made love again, naturally, but after, they could have snuggled on her couch, or gone for a walk... When she caught herself daydreaming about walking hand in hand beneath the blossom trees, she felt like smacking herself. What was she doing weaving fantasies about the man?

He had short-term written all over him. His cynical attitude toward wedding gifts and his stories about his father had made it clear Luke didn't see himself as a settling-down kind of guy. Not that she was looking to settle down, at least not right away. But she was a pretty traditional woman at heart. She wanted a home, a family, a dog, summer vacations at a beachfront cottage, backyard barbecues.

She sighed. The urge to settle, to nest, wasn't too strong yet, but it was there, and she knew it would gain strength in the next couple of years as thirty approached.

Well, she wasn't apologizing for who she was and what she wanted. As long as she kept her Luke fantasies in the bedroom, she'd be fine. But start thinking serious thoughts and she'd be doomed to disappointment.

It was strange to discover that it wasn't his sexual prowess, or lack thereof, that bothered her. She grinned at herself in the mirror as she brushed her teeth. Whew. That was some book he was reading. Even though he'd grilled her on her preferred techniques in the car, what his mouth had done with the information had been magic. He'd put his own interpretation on her preferences, and she'd liked it. She'd liked it very much.

She slapped on some makeup, slipped into a denim skirt, much shorter and tighter than the one she'd worn last night, squeezed herself into a red sleeveless tank top she'd rejected yesterday and stepped into black clogs. Her curls were still a little damp from the shower, but she let them go free, finger-combing them and letting them dry naturally. She'd look a little wilder than usual, but decided that suited her mood.

As Luke had reminded her at lunch, women sent messages all the time with their clothing. If he couldn't figure out she was broadcasting *Take me, baby,* to one very special man, then that man needed to have his eyes checked.

Luke's hair, unlike hers, appeared less wild than usual. He'd combed it off his face, but the tamed hair

only made the carnal expression in his eyes more apparent. He had *Take me, baby* written all over him,
too. He kissed her hello, after not seeing her for a full
hour, and she noticed he'd shaved. She also noticed
she didn't want to go out. She wanted to stay home
and get naked.

But she'd promised Therese she'd be at the party,
and she knew Therese needed the support. Chances
were Brad the Tongue was going to be there tonight.

"We'd better get going." She pulled away from
the kiss before it got totally out of control. Then she
dragged him out of the apartment.

On the way to the bon voyage party for Cliff and
Nadine Masters, she gave him a rundown of her close
friends. Therese would be there, and she couldn't wait
to find out what her friend thought of Luke when she
saw him in the flesh. Shari might be biased, but she
thought Luke would blow Therese's theory about
good-looking men out of the water.

Luke was both gorgeous in that careless way of his,
and a decent human being. He was also a star pupil
in the sex department. She couldn't wait to show him
off.

Shari and Luke pulled up outside a quiet older
home on Queen Anne Hill. The house was from the
late eighteen hundreds, before the gold-rush boom. It
was stately and solid and felt like a place where gen-
erations of families had grown up, where traditions
flourished. "I'd love a home like this someday," she
said.

Luke didn't reply. No doubt his idea of domestic
bliss was a one-person sailboat.

As they trod up the path, the heavy oak front door

opened and out flew Therese as fast as if the house were on fire.

She almost bolted past them without a glance before Shari stopped her. "Therese, it's me."

"*Cochon! Bête, bête, bête!*" Not only was her French giving away her agitation, Therese was also flushed and her royal-blue sweater was buttoned up all wrong.

Shari didn't have to reach far to find the likely cause of her friend's distress. "He's in there?"

A sharp nod was her answer. "He had the nerve to say to me…to say…" She threw up her hands and began ranting again. Shari's French might be a little rusty, but she recognized curses when she heard them.

Abruptly, Therese fell silent, and Shari got the feeling she'd only just noticed Luke. Her friend stared at him as if he were a pernicious insect she'd been called in to exterminate.

Rapidly, Shari made the introductions.

"Nice to meet you," said Luke, extending his hand.

"He's too good-looking," Therese said, ignoring Luke altogether. "Get rid of him now before he breaks your heart."

"Therese! Wait."

As Therese fled into the darkness, away from the house, Shari stood there helplessly.

"Don't worry about me," said Luke behind her. "If you want to go after her, go."

Even as she took a few tentative steps back up the path, she heard the roar of her friend's small sports car engine and knew she was too late.

"She needs time to cool off. Maybe she'll come

back.'' She hooked her hand through his arm. "But thanks for the offer.''

He kissed her quick and hard, and they headed up the stone steps and knocked on the door.

"Hi, Helen,'' Shari said when their hostess greeted them. Helen Boneville was the history teacher at the school. "This is my friend Luke.''

"Come on in.'' Helen hugged Shari and shook Luke's hand, eyeing him the way a mother hen would eye a fox checking out her chickens. Luke must have passed the inspection for she let them both in and told them to go have a good time.

"Wow,'' said Luke. "I almost didn't survive the first two of your friends. I'm scared to meet any more.''

Since most everyone knew each other, the party was pretty relaxed. With the odd exception, Shari liked all the other teachers.

She introduced Luke around, and was amused to see him being ruthlessly sized up by a couple of the older teachers who'd taken her under their wings when she'd first started at the high school. They were as bad as Helen.

She said her hellos as she moved through the kitchen to the living room, always keeping an eye out for the man who'd broken her best friend's heart.

Since he was the only man in the house she didn't know, and he fit Therese's description, she knew she'd found Brad Koslowski when she peeked into the study where a group of men had gathered. He sat in a leather recliner, but he wasn't reclining. He also wasn't taking part in the general conversation about the Mariners chances this year.

On studying him, Shari decided that Therese hadn't lied about his looks. You'd pass over him in a crowd. His hair was trimmed close to his balding head. His features were unremarkable and, while he was clearly athletic, he wasn't a large man.

He wore an abstracted expression and he tapped the beer bottle he was holding distractedly against his knee.

She wanted to hate him on sight for what he'd done to Therese, except that he looked sort of…lonely. Hmm. She wondered where Miss Swedish Pancakes was tonight.

Luke came up behind her, passed her a glass of wine and, seeing where her gaze was directed, sent her a quick smile. He then joined the group of baseball enthusiasts, bonding instantly as men seemed to do over sports.

Well, she couldn't stand here all night staring at the guy who'd broken her friend's heart. She hadn't decided whether to introduce herself or to simply back out of the room when the man in the chair glanced up at her. He had remarkable eyes, she thought, wondering if that's what had first attracted her friend. They were pale blue-gray with a dark ring around the iris. And they were staring right at her.

Seemed the decision was made. She couldn't beat a retreat now, so she decided to move forward and to introduce herself.

"You must be the new phys ed teacher," she said with cool politeness. "I'm Shari Wilson. I teach English."

They shook hands.

"I'm guessing you're also good friends with Therese."

Her eyes widened. "How do you know?"

"Because, apart from Therese, no one else looks as if they want to hurt me."

Well, since he'd waded right into the subject, she wasn't going to back down from it. "You're right. We're very close friends." *As in, I know what a sleaze you are, buddy.*

He nodded. Glancing at her as though considering what to say next, he dropped his gaze to his beer and said in a low, intense tone, "I want her back."

Oh, good. Nice start to a polite conversation between strangers. She almost laughed. If that wasn't exactly like a man. Stomp on a woman's heart and then expect her to bounce back into his arms with a snap of his fingers.

"I don't think that's going to happen," she said.

His head flopped back and he stared at the ceiling. "I applied for this job the second I heard about the opening. I figured it was fate."

Fate or a pathetic excuse to win back a woman who no longer wanted him. "I don't think Therese gives second chances."

"Look, I don't know how much she's told you, but I screwed up. I didn't realize I loved her until it was too late." His forehead wrinkled in concentration. "No. I don't think that's true. I think it was when I realized I loved her that I panicked and ran out on our relationship."

Oh, hand out the hankies. "You could have tried contacting her."

He glanced at her in surprise, those marvelous silver eyes burning with intensity. "I did. I called, e-mailed, showed up at her door. She accused me of stalking her and threatened to get a restraining order."

She almost smiled. When Therese was mad, watch out!

He shrugged. "I gave up. Until I saw this job posting. She's going to have to get used to me being around again. I only hope it's not too late."

If Therese hadn't admitted to loving this man, Shari would probably leave him stewing in the mess of his own making. But she'd never seen Therese so intense about any other guy. And, even though Shari had just met Brad, he didn't strike her as the type to pour out his heart to every stranger he met. "You've got to expect her to be angry. And I don't think she's thrilled that you're working at the same school."

His laugh was low and bitter. "I don't want to make things worse for her. I didn't expect her to kiss me hello, but I thought we could be civil at least. I guess I was wrong."

Shari was thinking fast. She couldn't betray Therese's confidence in any way, but perhaps there was a very slim chance that Therese and Brad could start fresh. What they did with their fresh start was up to them. Only one idea seemed to have any merit. "Tell her you just want to be friends."

"What? Why would I do that? I love her."

"She's angry with you." She shot him a glance from under her lashes. "With good cause. But she knows she's got to work with you, too." She also thought Therese was terrified of falling back in love with Brad, but she didn't say so. Her loyalty belonged to Therese. However, if there was any hope of a romance rekindling, it would take time. And if no kindling occurred, it would be easier on everyone concerned if the parties could be friends.

"That's my advice. Think about it at least. She's not going to go out with you again, but she might consider being friends."

Shari knew Therese pretty well. If she decided to let Brad back into her life, she was going to want more than friends. But it might do both of them good to get to know each other outside the bedroom before jumping right back in where they'd left off.

Brad was staring at her as though perhaps he was a mind reader as well as an amateur athlete. "You might just be on to something there. Thanks."

"What were you and the guy on the recliner plotting?" Luke asked on the way home.

"Not plotting. He broke Therese's heart, and I suggested instead of trying to get her back romantically, he should settle for being friends."

"Honey, no man who wants to have sex with a woman is going to be happy being her friend."

She shot him a surprised look. "It may interest you to know that that works both ways. I suspect that being friends first this time may make them better lovers."

Luke's hand reached for hers. "I found the opposite with you. Now that we're lovers, I'm liking you better all the time."

She laughed, but she thought there was a lot of truth in what he said. It wasn't just sex with her and Luke. They were becoming friends.

They were also neighbors.

Neighbors, friends and lovers.

She wondered how long they could stay all three.

16

SWEAT ROLLED DOWN Shari's throat and tickled before hitting the already damp neck of her gray cotton tank top. Amanda Marshall pounded in her ears through the earpiece of her Walkman as she pedaled up an impossibly steep hill while her stationary bike added insult to injury by going nowhere.

With only a week to go before the wedding, Shari was fiercely focused on her exercise program. Although, in truth, she was really liking the way the extra workouts made her feel. And now that she was getting naked with Luke on a regular basis, a little tighter muscle tone was a good thing.

She stared at her own perspiring reflection in the mirrors of their apartment building's grandiosely named Fitness Spa. The spa consisted of this room, with its one bike, universal gym and a smattering of free weights, a small sauna, and washrooms.

Luke was a man who liked to see what he was doing. He enjoyed making love to her in patches of sunlight, with the bedroom lights burning, in candlelight—anything but darkness. At first she'd assumed it helped him follow the book's instructions, but now she suspected he just liked looking at her naked.

She pedaled faster.

If it weren't for the mirrors she wouldn't have realized she had company. She saw movement and turned her head to see Luke stroll in with a casual wave in her direction.

He'd known she'd be here tonight because she'd told him, so he obviously wasn't surprised to see her. She, however, was quite surprised to see him.

He had a towel draped around his neck, and was wearing black workout shorts and a ratty old T-shirt with a rip under one arm.

His hair was in its usual disarray, looking as though he'd just crawled out of bed, but she was beginning to think the mess was from running his hands through it while he worked. Also, like her, he had a stubborn natural curl that needed time and styling products to achieve a decent style. The only hair-care product he used was shampoo. His styling involved a vigorous toweling after which he just left his hair to dry. She didn't think a comb ever got involved in the process.

Ridiculous that his tumbled, tangled hair should look so sexy, but it did.

She didn't slow her pedaling or remove the earphones, too suspicious of his coincidental appearance to want to encourage him. But, after that single wave, he ignored her and headed for the universal gym.

It was strange to have company while she worked out here. Not many residents used the facility. If they were into gym workouts, they mostly went to the bigger, glossier gyms down the road that offered acres of equipment, nonstop classes and personal instruction. She didn't come in here herself all that often, and she rarely saw anyone else when she did. So it was suspiciously odd that Luke had suddenly decided to work out here. Still, maybe he came every day. She didn't know for sure that he didn't—he'd simply never mentioned it.

Anyway, he gave her something to look at besides herself sweating in the mirror.

He was leaning back on a narrow, black-vinyl bench, pushing the weight bar from his chest to the full extension of his arms. She loved watching the fierce concentration of his face, the muscles bunch and stretch in his arms and the expansion and contraction of his chest as he breathed.

She watched him work his way around the apparatus in an obvious routine, so maybe he did use the gym on a regular basis.

After half an hour he'd almost completed a second circuit and her preprogrammed cycle was over. She pedaled idly as her breathing returned to normal.

She felt warm and loosened up. Warm everywhere in fact, as she watched Luke. Oh, that man had a body on him. She was thinking she'd give them both an extra workout. She'd invite him up to her place later.

She pulled her earpiece out and said, with what she hoped was nonchalance, "What are you doing later?"

He glanced at her from upside down, his quad muscles bulging as he hoisted weight up and down with his feet. "Why?"

She sent him as sexy a look as she could manage with sweat-damp tendrils of hair in her face and her clothes sticking to her. She glugged some water to clear her dry throat before answering. "I was thinking I'd shower and slip into something more comfortable."

He settled the weights back in their cradle with a metallic click and rolled to standing. He moved to-

ward her with a panther's easy grace, and she felt
desire snake through her belly along with a quiver of
uncertainty.

"I like you sweaty," he said and, reaching out a
hand, traced his index finger slowly across her chest
where her breasts swelled lightly over the neck of her
tank top. Her skin was damp and extrasensitive from
her workout and she sucked in a sharp breath as she
felt the slight roughness of his finger track its slow
path. She watched them in the mirror, mesmerized,
and saw her nipples pebble against the damp cotton
almost before she felt the tingling, tightening sensation. His gaze glued to hers in the mirror, he put his
finger in his mouth and sucked it.

A shudder went through her.

"I definitely like you sweaty," he said in a low
husky voice before blocking out her reflection by
claiming her mouth.

She tasted the salt of perspiration. Hers? His? Mingled, probably. Their lips were slick with it, and as
he rubbed his lips back and forth against hers, she felt
an urgent wave of desire swamp her.

She clutched at him and felt the heat coming off
his body through the warm, damp T-shirt, then his
hot damp skin as her fingers found the rip in his shirt.

He kissed her jaw, ran his lips down her throat, and
she watched in the mirror through half-slitted eyes.
His head was so dark against her white throat.

Desire was already clouding her senses and it must
have slowed her reflexes, because before she could
stop him, he grasped the hem of her shirt and yanked
it high, revealing her black sports bra.

"No. You can't," she mumbled. "Somebody could come."

He grinned at her with pure devilry. "Somebody's going to. That I promise."

And he flipped up the sports bra, baring her breasts to the brightly lit room, the mirror and any apartment resident who came through the door.

"I meant—" she gasped "—anyone could come in and see me…see us." He took a nipple into his mouth and she moaned.

"That's right," he said, the words reverberating against her flesh. "Anyone could come in and see us."

She wasn't an exhibitionist! She couldn't imagine anything more mortifying. A low moan escaped her throat as he pulled the other nipple into his mouth and she saw the first in the mirror, as glossy and red as candied fruit.

He was bent awkwardly to avoid the bike's handlebars, but he didn't seem to notice. She could hear the lap of his tongue against her breasts and the soft sighs coming from her own lips.

When he moved to stand behind her, she watched him cautiously, but still jumped when he put both arms around her, then pulled her back so she was still sitting on the bike, but leaning against his belly. In the mirror she saw herself, half-naked, gleaming with sweat. Saw his hand cup her belly then disappear under the waistband of her shorts.

"I want you to watch yourself come," he whispered in her ear.

"No, I…" But then he was touching her and conscious thought fled. She was hot and wet and sweaty and untidy and she couldn't possibly make such a spectacle of herself. Anyone could come in...

Dimly, she knew she could flip her top back down and get Luke's hand out of her pants pretty quickly, but not quickly enough to prevent any apartment resident in her building from seeing her like this.

His fingers moved rhythmically, hypnotically, taking her to a place where convention didn't matter. Her breasts rose and fell as her breathing grew labored, her nipples bouncing lightly as though caressed by an unseen hand.

He rubbed at her exquisitely sensitive, slippery flesh, hot from the workout, hot from embarrassment, hot from desire. She felt his fingers separating her folds to touch the rapidly beating heart of her.

In the mirror she saw him watching her, saw a face that was hers and yet not hers, so sultry and sensual, her lips impossibly plump and red, her eyes huge and unfocused, her cheeks flushed, damp tendrils of hair curling over her forehead and temples and cheeks.

"Anyone could walk in," he repeated. "They'd see you like this, spread out in all your glory, being pleasured."

She moaned, and her moan turned into a cry as he plunged two fingers deep inside her. Her hips rode that bike furiously as intense sensation built, layer by layer. She'd never felt so vulnerable, or so open, watching him watching her. Seeing her own abandoned pleasure.

"Oh, I'm going to... Oh." The rest of her words were lost, drowned by the wave that rose suddenly from within, its roar deafening her. She tried to close her eyes, but he wouldn't let her. His free hand pulled her chin forward and she was so startled her eyes snapped open and she watched herself in the throes of a powerful orgasm.

She was shocked at how wild she looked and sounded. Her mouth was open on a sigh, her face tight with concentration and flushed with passion.

"You are so beautiful when you come," he told her, staying with her through the aftershocks. "I wanted you to see it."

Suddenly he spun her, throwing her off balance physically and emotionally yet again. From somewhere a condom appeared and then she knew what she'd suspected—he'd planned this all along.

He scooped her up and walked with her to the black workbench and laid her on it. He took her hands and wrapped her fingers around the black-vinyl handles, as though she were going to bench-press the weights. "Hang on."

He brushed aside her feeble protest as easily as one leg of her wide-legged exercise shorts, scooping her panties out of the way at the same time. While she was still flustered and thinking they should go up to her apartment before they really were discovered, he pulled her hips to the edge of the bench press, told her to put her feet on his shoulders and thrust inside her in one long motion.

The tail end of her climax still quivered within her and it was as though her sensitive flesh were being stroked from the inside; new tingles radiated. He thrust hard, and fast. She clutched the handles for balance as her body tossed and rocked on the narrow bench. He half squatted in front of her, holding on to her knees as he thrust rhythmically into her. Her hips rocked right off the vinyl to meet him. She felt the bulge of the same quad muscles she'd watched earlier. She loved his strength and control, although he was fast approaching loss of control. She thought she'd watch him as he'd watched her, enjoy the helpless openness of his expression at the moment of total release, but then he stroked her. She'd have thought she'd be too tender to be touched again so soon on that hottest of hot spots, but it was barely a flutter of pressure, and her own wetness almost soothed even as his gentle touch excited her all over again.

She wanted to hang on to control this time, but it was too much. When he took her mouth she opened to him. She wrapped her legs around his hips, and her back bent until her shoulder blades jammed against the bench. She was dimly aware that she was getting a second workout tonight, and then his strokes increased in speed and urgency. His fingers insisted she respond, and she couldn't help herself. As he stiffened, then bucked against her, her legs squeezed him tight, tight, tight against her and she cried out her ecstasy into his mouth.

It took several minutes for her to come back to earth, but when she did she found him grinning at her, a totally smug expression on his face.

"I think I'm a damn good personal trainer if I do say so myself."

She rolled her gaze and pushed him away so she could pull her clothing back into order.

He disappeared into the bathroom and came back to say, "Feel like a sauna?"

"It takes half an hour to warm up."

"I was thinking our own natural body heat would do the trick."

"I think all my exhibitionism is over for the night. Anyway, now I definitely need a shower."

"No problem, there's one right here. Plenty of room for two."

She glared at him, trying not to fall for his charm, but her lips couldn't stop trying to smile. "No. Upstairs."

He put on a hopeful-puppy look. "Do I get to join you?"

She thought about it for a full second. "Yes."

It was a very long, soapy shower.

THE FIRST THING that struck Luke when he pushed through the scratched and dented front door of the high school was the smell. It was as if he were going back in time. He'd forgotten that mix of adolescent sweat, chalk dust and cleaning chemicals that sent him traveling through time to feel like a high school troublemaker again.

A kid half a foot taller than him with sneakers the size of Montana gave him a curious once-over as Luke stood there taking it all in—a glass case containing athletic trophies, a plaque with the names of the top scholastic achievers, the patches of fresh paint on the buff walls that didn't quite cover scrawled black graffiti.

Luke shook his head and followed Shari's directions to the office. He hadn't quite reached it when the bell rang and the relative quiet was over. Chairs scraped, voices rose, doors opened and streams of kids spilled out into the hallway.

He dodged bodies and curious glances and finally escaped into the office where he asked a surly receptionist who looked as though she ate freshmen for coffee break to page Shari. It seemed touch-and-go as to whether she would or not, and Luke realized his palms were sweating. He wouldn't go back to high school for a million bucks.

He had to stifle the urge to kiss Shari when he saw her. Even though they'd made love that morning, she shook his hand, darting a glance at the old biddy receptionist as she did so. It seemed to him that her blush would broadcast to the world that they were beyond the hand-shaking stage, but if pretending they were strangers gave her confidence, he was happy to play along. He'd tease the hell out of her later, though.

"Well," she said breathlessly, "you're right on time. Come to my classroom and we'll get you set up."

"Thank you, Ms. Wilson," he said.

God, she was cute when she was flustered. "Please, you can call me Shari."

She waited until they were in her classroom to say another word. "I'm sure that old gossip suspected something the way you were looking at me."

"Shari, we were at that party together with a bunch of teachers. I think they know something's up."

"You don't understand. Miss Pavel is the last person you ever want to know about your business. Believe me. She'd carry on forever if she thought I had a boyfriend."

Luke was amazed at the sharp burst of hurt pride

he felt. He wanted Shari telling Miss Pavel and every-one else in the world that he and she were a couple.

He blinked at his own thoughts.

He did?

Pushing all ideas about their relationship, whatever it was, to the back of his mind, he pulled out his notes and put them in the right order.

"Do you have everything you need?" Shari asked him.

"Not quite," he said, and kissed her swiftly.

She pulled away, her color high once more. "That is completely against school regulations," she said on a laugh.

"I'll get the rest of that after school," he promised them both.

Before she could reply—if she was even going to—the first kids shuffled into the room. He blinked as the desks filled rapidly and noisily. It was as though he were looking back at his own high school class. Apart from the change in fashions, the kids were the same. He could pick out the smart ones, the nerds, the athletes and the rebels. Amazing.

He felt a wave of protectiveness that Shari should be alone with this pack of wild animals every day. Then the bell rang and she moved to stand in front of the scarred oak desk. Silence fell like a stage curtain.

"Class, this is Mr. Lawson. He's going to talk to us about working on a newspaper."

He would have asked them to call him Luke, but she'd already warned him about that. Mr. Lawson wasn't him, that was his father, but he figured he could impersonate Mr. Lawson for Shari one day out of his life. He impersonated a total moron every day. He shrugged off the thought uncomfortably, cleared his throat and said, "Hi." He looked around at the faces staring at him with a variety of expressions from bored to catatonic, and remembered what it was like to sit in classes day after day listening to boring stiffs like him.

He glanced at his neat pile of notes. Hell with it.

"Who, what, when, where, why. These are the building blocks of a newspaper article." He stepped to the blackboard and wrote the five words down, the scratch of chalk and the smell of the dusty eraser so familiar.

He turned to stare at the class. The class stared back. Boredom was changing to puzzlement. Progress.

"So, let's build a story. Tell me something that's going on at this school that we can turn into a story."

Silence.

A jock-looking type at the back hauled a designer sneaker onto his desk and retied the lace.

"You, with your foot on the desk. What's your name?"

The athletic foot clonked to the lino. "Eddie."

"Eddie, tell me something that's going on. Any of your teams winning?"

The kid slumped in his seat. "Yeah."

"Which team?"

"The football team."

"The Orcas," piped up one of the keeners.

Luke turned back to the board. Circled *who* and wrote, "The Orcas." It took a few minutes and more tooth-pulling than an orthodontist did, but soon he had a lead paragraph. "The Orcas, Seattle Middle High's football A team, beat the Tigers at their home field Wednesday night."

"That's great," said Luke, noting the kids were a lot more interested now the stories were about them. "What else is happening? Let's do another one."

"Milo over in the corner can't get to first base with Rena Drummond."

Among the general juvenile snickering, Luke rolled his eyes in Shari's direction. "Enough sports stories. How about hard news? Safety issues? Overcrowding in the classrooms?" He turned and challenged them. "What do you guys want that you aren't getting?"

"New tennis courts."

"Computer lab time."

A hand went up in the corner.

"Yeah?" Luke acknowledged the girl.

"My assistance dog."

"What kind of assistance dog?"

"I don't walk very well. But the school only allows seeing-eye dogs. They won't let me bring Daisy to school."

"I like this one. A human interest story, and maybe, if we go public with this, we can get the rules changed for you. It's worth a try." He glanced around the class. "So, what's our lead?"

Shari hadn't been certain how Luke would do with her students, and had secretly prepared some backup questions and information about journalism of her own in case he flopped. But gazing at the eager faces and the raised hands, the general excitement in the room as the kids and Luke worked together to write a news story, she accepted he'd surprised her yet again.

With her help, Luke Lawson was turning into the confident, sexy, charismatic man she'd thought he was when they'd first met over mixed mail. The fact that she was part of his journey filled her with warmth.

Her students were so excited and enthused, she had a feeling that if the story found its way into the local paper, Lori was going to get her dog in school, after all.

And, as the kids would say, that was *sweet*.

17

AN ODD BLEND of nerves and excitement swirled inside Shari to the same rhythm that her purple silky hem swirled around her legs as she shifted in front of the dressing mirror in her bedroom. Sun spilled into her window. It looked as though B.J. was going to have a beautiful day for her wedding. After a month of hard work Shari was ready to face the day. In fact, she ought to thank B.J. If it hadn't been for her, Shari wouldn't have ended up becoming intimate with Luke, and she couldn't imagine now what it would be like not to have him in her life.

She twirled once more in front of the mirror. The bold purple dress was perfect. One of those bland pastels would have made her feel like a woman trying to fit in with the rest of the crowd. The woman in the mirror set her own style, with the bright dress, strappy sandals and colorful shawl. She'd styled her hair in long, loose curls and put extra effort into her makeup. All that working out had given her tighter muscles but also a glow of health. She looked her best and knew it.

When her doorbell rang, she was ready even though Luke was a couple of minutes early.

She opened the door and nearly fell over. She wasn't the only one who'd gone to extra effort with their appearance. Luke wore a summer-weight gray suit that had "designer" written all over it, but discreetly—in small letters. Under it he wore a crisp white shirt saved from being dull by a tie patterned in crayon-colored zigzags.

He'd had his hair cut and styled; he was clean-shaven. She thought he looked gorgeous when he was slopping around in jeans and two-day stubble. Dressed up he made her tongue hang out. "I thought you were wearing a tux."

"Too hot. Besides, they might make a mistake and accidentally marry me to B.J."

"I like the tie." Secretly she thought he couldn't look better in a tuxedo.

"Thanks." He stepped closer and every neuron in her body snapped to attention. How did he do that to her so effortlessly? "You look so good in that dress, all I want to do is take it off."

She giggled and stepped back. "Play your cards right and maybe later you'll get a chance."

The look he sent her said there'd be no chance about it. "I got you something," he said and, digging into his pocket pulled out a small square box wrapped in silver paper.

Her brows rose as she took it. She tore off the wrapping and opened the white box with the name of a Belltown jeweler stamped on the front in gold. Inside was a silver necklace with square tiles in a flowing mosaic of purple, red and yellow, and earrings to match.

"Oh, they're gorgeous!" she cried, her hand flying to her bare throat. She hadn't been able to find jewelry to match her dress and wrap, but this set was perfect.

She held them against the shawl and the color match was almost uncanny.

"Wherever did you find them?"

"A jeweler I know."

She removed the silver drop earrings she was wearing, and put on the new ones. Then she held out the necklace to Luke.

He stepped behind her. "Lift your hair." His voice was soft and sensuous, whispering against her hair. Her skin prickled as she complied, her own curls feeling sensuous as they tumbled over her hands and wrists. He fastened the clasp and his fingertips brushed the back of her neck, making her shiver. Before she dropped her hair he placed a quick kiss on her nape.

She almost danced to her bedroom to check out the new jewelry in the mirror. She struck a pose with the shawl, and suddenly remembered how she'd left the bag with her dress and shawl in his car overnight when they'd been in such a hurry to get to chapter seven.

She hadn't retrieved them until the following afternoon. He must have taken the shawl with him to search for... Her fingers rose to her throat to touch the cheerful links, again noting they weren't merely a close match to the colors in the shawl, but an exact match. Had he had the pieces specially made?

It was such a sweet, thoughtful gesture, and the fact that he wasn't boasting about his thoughtfulness made it all the sweeter.

He was, she was beginning to think, a keeper. Now she simply had to get him believing it.

"These are so perfect," she said as she waltzed

back out of her bedroom. "Thanks." And she kissed him until her own toes curled.

"Well? Are you ready to face B.J. and friends?" she asked.

"One devoted love slave coming up," he said, and held out his hand for hers.

As they drove to the wedding she said, "I liked your feature in the weekend paper, by the way." She'd read it this morning with her breakfast and chuckled all the way through, imagining Luke on assignment.

He groaned. "I never, ever thought I'd write an article that included the benefits of breast milk. Hell, I never wanted to know what Montgomery's Tubules were. Now I'll never look at a breast in the same way."

She laughed.

"No, really. I'm serious. Let's pull over and I'll show you. Your naked breasts will inspire nothing but a learned opinion on their perfection as 'receptacles of nourishment,'" he said, quoting his article.

"How did you end up doing it?" It wasn't at all his usual type of article, though she had to hand it to him, he'd done a pretty good job of getting the breast-feeding club's points across, without sounding like a guy. He'd written about everything from the natural antibodies in breast milk to inverted nipples, and managed to do it with a certain dignity. But she couldn't imagine why the paper hadn't assigned a woman for the job.

"The truth is kind of embarrassing."

"Luke, you fainted at the sight of my naked body. I think we're beyond embarrassing."

He sighed. "You're never going to forget that, are you?"

"No."

"Well, the two are sort of related."

She bit her lip and turned to him. "You didn't faint at the breast-feeding meeting?"

"Pass out. And, no. I didn't. I agreed to do that article in exchange for taking your class on a tour of the paper."

She opened her mouth and then couldn't think of a thing to say. Her lips formed a silent *O*.

"I was sure you were going to dump me on my sorry ass after I had that little blood sugar episode. It was lame and pathetic, but that school tour was my best shot at keeping you still speaking to me."

She didn't say a word and he shot her a mocking expression. "Well? Am I right?"

She nodded. "Luke?"

"Mmm?"

"I'm glad you did the breast-feeding article. And the kids are so excited about touring your paper they're working really hard on their articles, hoping they get a chance to be in print. You did a great job with them."

"It was fun."

She couldn't believe how close she'd come to pulling the plug on their own deal. She'd have missed getting to know Luke better and, worst of all, she'd have missed becoming intimate with him. Maybe their lovemaking wasn't as technically smooth as it would ultimately be, but they were avid students of that silly book of Luke's. It was getting to the point where the sight of that garish red-and-black cover made her wet. And, advanced technique was great, but there was a lot to be said for raw enthusiasm, which was overflowing in Luke.

"I'm glad, too," he said at last.

Since Luke was a good driver and she was a good navigator, they got to the church in plenty of time.

She'd wondered how she'd feel when she saw B.J. again. It had been a couple of years since Shari had seen her, and more like five since she'd seen Randy.

When she saw her college boyfriend waiting at the top of the aisle, she wondered why her heart had been broken over him. He was all right, but nothing special. Then the music started and they all rose. After the parade of bridesmaids, B.J. walked slowly toward him in a wedding gown right out of *Martha Stewart Weddings*.

Shari didn't feel the anguish and hurt she'd expected the day would resurrect; she suddenly saw B.J. as the scrawny twelve-year-old she'd been when they first met. Then she had flashes of them as friends in high school and as dorm mates in college. She wasn't going to pretend that it hadn't hurt to have a close friend and her boyfriend abandon her for each other, but the fact they were still together and getting married mitigated the severity of their crime. Somewhat.

Walt Whitman must have really done a number on them, for they were clearly in love with each other. How wonderful it must be to get married to the man you knew was your forever guy.

She reached for Luke's hand simply because she wanted to feel the warmth and weight of his hand in hers.

The necklace he'd bought her lay smooth against

her throat. He wasn't the kind of man who was so busy climbing a corporate ladder he didn't have time for the people he cared about in his life.

Quite the opposite in fact. He obviously worked hard and had enough drive and self-discipline to write a novel, but he also took time out to smell the roses. And send roses, she mused, remembering her surprise when she'd first received them. Since they'd become lovers he was always showing up with flowers.

And he'd put a lot of thought and care into choosing or, more likely, having designed, the jewelry she was wearing today.

Maybe it was attending a wedding ceremony that was making her mushy, but she suddenly saw Luke as the kind of man she could marry. He'd be great with kids, too, she realized, recalling how good he'd been with the teens in her class.

The blond-oak pews creaked in unison as the wedding guests resumed their seats once the bride reached the groom.

Shari sat there, surprisingly moved to watch two old friends getting married. A lot of her residual humiliation evaporated as it finally occurred to her that they really did love each other. At least she hadn't been dumped for a two-week fling.

Luke kept her hand in his, and she remained aware of the constant warm connection between them as the ancient words of the marriage ceremony echoed in the church.

One day it would be her turn and, as her gaze dropped instinctively to their linked hands, she realized that it was Luke she wanted to marry.

Her eyes widened in shock as the truth hit her. If

she wanted to marry him then she must be…she must be… Oh, Lord. She was in love with him.

The knowledge made her feel warm all over.

Tears trembled on her lashes and spilled over during the marriage ceremony. They were tears of happiness, but not for B.J. and Randy. They were for herself. She was in love. And she'd found the man she wanted to spend the rest of her life with.

Once they got to the reception at a snooty golf club, Luke kept his part of their original bargain. "You do a great job pretending to be my devoted love slave," she told him laughingly as he brought her a glass of champagne and kissed her hand.

His eyes laughed right back at her, but his words were seriously sexual. "I *am* your devoted love slave."

Her breath caught as he cupped her cheek and kissed her lightly, murmuring, "I'll prove it when we get home."

Whether it was his teasing words that put her on simmer or her newfound knowledge that she'd fallen in love with him, she didn't know, but desire bubbled constantly as she chatted with old friends and introduced Luke to them.

With smug pride, she noted that he was quite a hit. And as a love slave he wasn't bad, either. Throughout dinner, he took every possible opportunity to touch her, whether with a nudge of his knee under the table or a caressing finger down her cheek or his arm thrown seemingly carelessly along the back of her chair so his fingers just touched her bare shoulder.

She knew it was deliberate. She knew it was extended foreplay. She suspected it came straight out of that damn book of his. It didn't matter; he was driving her absolutely wild with lust.

She hoped he'd had a recent physical, for she was planning to retaliate when they returned home, and he'd need all his strength to keep up with her.

After the speeches, which she barely heard over the sound of her own blood roaring in her ears, they watched B.J. and Randy enjoy their first dance as a married couple.

"I can't believe you broke your heart over that guy," Luke said.

"What can I say? I was young and foolish." She turned to Luke and patted his cheek. "I have much better taste now."

"Let's dance," he said when the floor was opened to everyone.

She melted against him and found he danced with the easy athletic grace he did most things. She moved with him instinctively, and she imagined anyone watching them would immediately know they were lovers.

It was heaven to be with him, to smell his scent when she laid her cheek on his shoulder, to know that soon she'd be in his arms making love.

As though he'd read her thoughts, he said, "We're getting out of here."

"But we can't. It would be rude to leave before the bride and groom."

"Consider it payback time for *Leaves of Grass*."

"I don't think—"

"I need to be inside you. Badly."

A tiny, helpless moan was surprised out of her. What were social manners when set against this kind of burning, physical need? "I'll pretend I'm going to the washroom. You head for the bar, and we'll meet at the car."

"Got it."

They snuck out of the country club parking lot like a pair of criminals.

"Do you think they'll notice we snuck out?"

"Do you care?"

If her choice was between socializing with people she hadn't seen in years or making love with Luke, there was really no contest.

She replied by leaning across the seat and tracing the curve of his ear with her tongue. "No. I really don't care."

"Grab the map out of the glove compartment," he said urgently.

"Why?"

"There must be a shortcut to get home."

18

"I'VE GOT SOME GREAT NEWS, Luke," Matthew Hargreaves, his agent, bellowed from New York.

"What is it?" Luke asked blearily, blinking and trying to find the clock so he could confirm that it was much too early to be awake and talking to anybody.

His agent always forgot the time difference to the West Coast, despite repeated reminders from Luke, who'd been awake long after Shari had fallen asleep in his arms last night. He'd never spent a weekend like it. They'd barely left his bed since coming home from the wedding Saturday night.

They'd made a game of the advanced positions in the latter chapters of the book, trying out every single one. It had been magical, funny, searingly sexual and scary as hell.

He'd finally snuck out of bed around three this morning. Not wanting to wake her, he'd bypassed the computer and grabbed paper and a pen and taken them out to the couch in his living room.

It had been a waste of time. He couldn't write.

He'd paced.

If he'd been a smoker, he'd have puffed through a pack, one cigarette after another. If he'd been directing the scene, he'd have called for black and white and a solo sax wailing in the background. That's what kind of a night it had been, what kind of a mood he'd been in.

Shari's scent was on his skin just as surely as she was sleeping in his bed. Every time he caught a whiff of her fragrance, or thought about her, he felt both panicky and relieved; in terrible danger and yet more secure than ever before.

Something was different about the way he was with this woman than he'd been with any other.

He was very much afraid that something was love.

Halting his pacing to stare blearily out his window at the first streaks of dawn over Mount Rainier, he wondered, Was this what happened to his father? Time after time?

Could Luke be different? Or was he merely starting on the path to letting women down later?

How could he tell?

He'd crawled back into bed a few minutes before six-thirty, because he'd wanted to be there when she woke. He loved watching Shari wake up. This morning he'd watched her eyes blink the minute the alarm went off, then she'd eased back for a full-bodied stretch. Next she kissed him, and he'd realized he was kissing her for the first time knowing he was in love with her. He'd pulled her flush against him and tried to tell her with his body what he couldn't yet say in words.

"Stop, or I'll be late," she giggled, then rolled out of bed and whispered to him to go back to sleep.

Amazingly, he did, feeling a sense of contentment that was both new and welcome.

Now he blinked again, forcing himself to concentrate on his agent's words. He hauled himself up to a sitting position and snapped on a light. He'd sent his novel to Matthew to read. Had he looked at it already? Did he like it? Luke wasn't normally nervous about his work, but this book meant something to him.

"Hey, Luke. You still there?" Matthew's voice dragged him back to his search for the time. Not quite seven. Well, it wasn't that bad. He was usually up by now, but he was functioning on so little sleep it felt like the wee hours.

"Yeah, I'm here. What's the news?"

"Ginger." Matthew stretched the word out like saltwater taffy, treating each syllable as though it were a complete word. "Gin. Ger."

Silence. What on earth was the man talking about?

"She wants you on her show."

"Oh, that Ginger." He made the connection. Daytime talk show woman. Right. He yawned, and moved his neck around to get the kinks out. Chapter twelve should come with a chiropractic warning.

"What is your problem today? There *is* only one Ginger. And she reaches a core viewing public of a couple million every day. I sent in your sex book. She wants you. Next week. You fly down to L.A. Tuesday, appear on the show Wednesday."

"You've been conned, Matt. They book those things months ahead." All Luke wanted to do was to go back to sleep. He wondered vaguely if Matthew had taken up drinking.

There was a short pause. "I'm going to level with you, Luke. She had another one of my authors scheduled. Guy did a prima donna act and now he's not doing the show.''

Luke rolled his eyes. ''So it's me you need a favor from. You want to slot me in a vacant spot.''

''It's still the opportunity of a lifetime. I've already contacted your publisher. They're salivating. Already going back to press on *Total Morons*. This is huge, my friend. Huge.''

Luke knew it was huge. If he wasn't so tired he'd probably be pretty excited. People who appeared on ''Ginger'' sold a lot of books. He'd pole-vault to the next level. But his gut wasn't happy. He scanned through all the reasons he didn't want to do the show, but there was really only one that sprang to mind— he didn't want Shari finding out. And that, of course, was that.

''I don't think so, Matt.''

There was a heavy sigh. ''I wish you'd think about it. It's a lot easier to sell a first novel from a writer who's got some credibility.''

Luke's eyes narrowed. ''What do you mean?''

''If you do the 'Ginger' show, millions of readers see you. They see you're a handsome guy, can string a few words together. Your how-to book becomes an instant bestseller. My job's a lot easier.''

Luke didn't consider himself more of a fool than the next man. He knew when he was getting the squeeze.

He might not be a native New Yorker like Matt, but he wasn't a total pushover, either. ''What did you think of the novel?''

''Pretty good.''

''Good enough to publish?''

There was another pause. Luke felt the weight of Matt's calculation as they played a delicate game on the phone. Lack of sleep was a definite handicap in his corner.

"I think it's good enough. In fact, I think it's great. Best thing you've ever done. But it's the publishers who decide these things."

And the agent who led the cheering section and hyped the manuscript.

"I want to send it out to a couple editors, see what they think."

Matthew didn't mention the word auction, but it reverberated down the phone lines with deafening clarity. If the book was good enough, and more than one publishing house wanted it badly enough, they'd bid against each other. An auction was a writer's dream, and Luke was as much a dreamer as the next lowly scribe.

"Of course, if I tell them you're going to be on 'Ginger' next week, they'll be salivating. I could call any of my writers with a book out, and they'll chop off limbs for the opportunity I'm giving you."

If it had just been the how-to book, Luke would have stayed firm, but the wily old devil had hooked him with his own novel. He'd do more than flog *Total Morons* if it meant a chance at getting *Prisons of the Mind* published.

He ran a hand across his stubbly chin, ignoring the tiny warning voice whispering in his ear that he ought to confess to Shari that he'd written *Sex for TMs* before revealing his identity to daytime-TV-watching America. But she worked all day and had too busy a life to spend much time in front of the television.

She'd never know he and Lance Flagstaff were one
and the same unless he told her. And he would tell
her, in his own time and in his own way.

He'd only discovered a couple of hours ago that he
was in love with the woman. He needed time to digest
the idea and work out what he was going to do with
the information before blabbing the truth about his
little experiment. For Shari's sake, now that he knew
he was in love with her, he should run like hell in the
opposite direction. But, selfishly, he wasn't certain he
could.

He hadn't been able to provide Jenkins, his cop
hero in *Prisons,* with a happy ending, and that was
fiction. How on earth did he think he could craft a
happily ever after with a real woman, given that his
own temperament and DNA were against him.

Luke shook his head. He needed more time. He'd
tell Shari he was the author of *TMs.* When the time
was right, he'd tell her.

SHARI SNEEZED for the seventh time in a row. Her
eyes were running and her nose sore from blowing.
Too much sex and not enough sleep must have weakened her system or something, but she'd caught the
flu that was going 'round the school, and caught it
hard.

Therese, who'd jumped back at the first nasal ex-
plosion, eyed her with disfavor. "This behavior may
be putting you in the running for martyr of the year,
but it's not doing our relationship any good. Go home
before everybody gets sick."

Shari nodded miserably. "I will. I need to pick up
the essays from my next class, then I'll go home."

"Good. Your boyfriend's home all the time. Get him to make you some hot soup or something."

Shari shook her head. "He had to go out of town on business."

"Business? You mean, for an article?"

In truth, Luke had been kind of vague. He told her it was connected to the novel she'd encouraged him to submit to his agent, but somehow she'd never ended up with the details.

She wished Luke was home. He wouldn't have shunned her like Therese. He'd have made her tea and tucked her into bed. Their love wasn't conditional on perfect health.

Her gasp of shock turned into a coughing fit that had her almost driving off the road.

Their *love?* They'd never said the word to each other—she hadn't even allowed herself to think he might return her sentiments—but she realized it was there, hovering like the invisible germs that had snuck into her body and turned into a full-blown cold. She loved him. And maybe, just maybe, he loved her right back.

She stopped at the drugstore on her way home and stocked up on cold remedies and tissue. On impulse, she bought herself a bunch of tulips from the flower vendor next door. If Luke were home, he'd bring her flowers.

When she let herself into the apartment, she went straight to her bedroom and changed into her warmest, snuggliest sweats, slipped into her fuzzy slippers and wrapped herself in Luke's terry-cloth robe. It had somehow ended up at her place and it was bigger than hers, so would be warmer, she told herself, bundling into it and letting it hug her. She wished she hadn't lost her sense of smell; she wanted to catch a whiff of Luke's scent from the garment.

She schlepped back out to the living area, glanced at the essays that needed marking, sniffed, felt her forehead and decided she was probably too feverish to work. She then looked at the television and figured she really needed rest.

Grabbing a pillow off her bed and the purple chenille throw from the back of her couch, she snuggled up and flipped on the TV.

A rerun of "Friends." *Flip.* Some kind of home blender on the home shopping channel. Hmm. Earrings coming up later, maybe she'd check back. *Flip.*

Cooking show. They were making a cream soup with lots of garlic. She wished somebody would offer her a bowl of homemade soup. If Luke were here he'd make her soup. What was the point of having a boyfriend who lived in the same apartment block and worked from home if he was going to go out of town the one day she came home sick and needed him? *Flip.*

"Ginger." Ah, Shari wasn't much into talk shows. Maybe she'd go back to see what Ross and Rachel were doing. She'd pop some meds, drink some herbal tea and go to bed.

She was about to flip back to "Friends," when Ginger said, with a knowing glance to the camera, "Is your man a total moron in bed? Don't give up hope. Maybe he can be trained to become a to-die-for lover. Our next guest is Lance Flagstaff, author of *Sex for Total Morons: A How-To Guide.*"

Huh. Shari forgot the meds and got comfortable.

This, she had to see. Who was this man who'd brought her and Luke together? His book might have been the thing that got Luke on the path to self-improvement, but she liked to think she'd had a lot to do with teaching him how to please a woman.

Smiling smugly, and wishing Luke were in town so they could watch this together, she ran to her VCR and stuck a blank tape in the machine and pushed the record button. It was a special book for them, she'd record this for Luke. With eager curiosity, she ran back to the couch and waited through the commercial break until Ginger's guest appeared.

He walked onto the stage, smiling broadly, giving a diffident wave to the bunch of hooting and clapping women, who seemed to make up the bulk of the audience.

He shook hands with Ginger as though they were old friends, then sat at ease in one of her pink armchairs.

"So, Lance," Ginger said with a let's-us-girls-have-some-fun glance at the audience, "you must be quite an expert in bed to teach other people how to be good lovers."

The camera zoomed in for a close-up shot of Lance's face.

A horrible gurgling sound came out of Shari's mouth.

Luke—her Luke—was on television. Promoting the book that he had written.

Sex for Total Morons: A How-To Guide. Ginger was holding it up for the world to see, that lurid red-and-black cover.

Oh, it had worked, all right. She wondered how

many other naive women he'd conned with that teach-me-to-love-you crap.

Hot color scalded her face as she thought about the way she'd guided him in the ways of pleasing her, guided him right into her body. And worst of all, into her heart.

She ought to slap the TV off, but she couldn't tear herself away. With horrified fascination, she watched this man she'd thought she'd known and discovered she didn't know at all.

Women in the audience were asking him questions, eager for their turn to ask him—Luke, Lance, whatever his name was—for advice.

Oh, he was charming, he was smooth, she'd give him that. She only wished Ginger had a phone-in line, because Shari had a question or two she'd like to ask Mr. Lance Flagstaff.

She was sniffing faster than her box of tissue could keep up and realized it wasn't just the cold; she was crying. Sobbing, damn it.

He'd betrayed her in the most basic way possible. Stolen her trust, posed as something he wasn't. He'd lied. Every time they'd climbed into bed and he'd hesitated, or had asked her what she liked, he'd been lying. He probably laughed himself silly every day at her expense.

"So, I have to tell you. I'm skeptical," Ginger said. She picked up the book and flapped it once more in front of the camera. "Can a book teach you how to be a good lover?"

The camera closed in on Luke, and the grin he sent Ginger was both teasing and self-deprecating.

"I wasn't sure of the answer to that myself when

I wrote the book, to be honest with you, Ginger. But I actually conducted an experiment in the last few weeks.''

"No," Shari whispered, curling into a fetal ball. "No."

"I've learned a lot since getting together with the woman I'm with now. I learned that every time you make love with someone new you have to learn their particular likes and dislikes, their unique responses. A caress that sends one woman straight to ecstasy may leave the next woman wishing she had her nail file handy to pass the time. Am I right?''

Here he glanced at the audience and was rewarded with delighted giggles and nodding heads.

"I think any book about making love and learning to give and receive pleasure is great. But it's only a guide. It gives some suggestions, some techniques and positions that might work. Try them out. But the most important thing is to talk to your partner. She's the expert on her own body. She knows what she likes and she'll help you become the best lover of her body that you can be. That's all that matters in the end.''

"So, Lance," Ginger said, "what's the number-one tip for being a knock-your-socks-off lover?''

Luke sighed, and appeared vaguely uncomfortable with the question for the first time since the interview had begun. Shari waited, barely breathing, for his answer, certain he was about to share some detail about their love life that she'd thought was private.

After a couple of seconds of silence, he said, "I know this sounds corny, but the very best, most mind-blowing sex happens when you're in love with your partner. I guess I wasn't much of an expert at all, because I just figured it out.''

"The best sex happens when you're in love with your partner. What do you all think of that?''

More hooting and clapping.

"Lance," said Ginger, "I think you might be on to something.''

A soggy tissue hit the TV screen in Shari's living room and bounced off, hitting the floor in a limp, white heap. Love? Did the man have even the most basic inkling of the concept?

Love was about sharing and honesty and support.

She blew her nose, turned off the television and unplugged the phone.

Love was about openness and trust. It wasn't about deceit and lies and *experiments*.

Luke was coming home tonight. The very last thing she intended was to see him.

LUKE WHISTLED as he approached the apartment building by cab from the airport. The scent of roses filled the air. He'd made the cabbie stop so he could buy the flowers from a street-side vendor.

He smiled wryly at his own symbolism. Everything was coming up roses in his life.

His agent was beside himself. The show had gone well, watched, Luke later found out, by two of the editors who were interested in his novel. Matthew had hinted at some competition among publishing houses interested in acquiring *Prisons of the Mind*.

Roses might be old-fashioned, but they had "proposal on bended knee" written all over them.

And he was feeling old-fashioned enough to drop at Shari's feet to ask her to be his wife. For he'd finally realized that he wasn't like his dad at all. If Luke had only loved once in twenty-eight years it seemed fair to assume his was the forever kind of love.

He couldn't wait to tell Shari.

He had a feeling he'd been using his father as an excuse all these years to avoid long-term relationships and anything that smacked of permanence. Now he'd fallen in love with Shari and he wanted her forever. Maybe his father had never grown up, but Luke felt as though he'd finally become an adult and accepted his adult feelings.

He'd sensed the truth of his emotions, then been manipulated into admitting them on television. Which should have freaked him. But the opposite had happened. Ever since he'd said the words on network TV he felt as if millions of viewers knew about his love before he'd told Shari, and that wasn't right.

In fact, a lot of his recent behavior wasn't right. He knew he had to explain it all to her. He didn't want to wait another minute.

He called her again, for about the twentieth time, but still there was no answer. Even her answering machine wasn't picking up. Maybe there was something wrong with her line.

It had crossed his mind to spend some of the money his agent assured him would be coming his way between the imminent sale of his novel and the extra royalties from having his book promoted on television. He'd been tempted, after his stint on the show was finished, to wander into a fancy Hollywood jeweler's and pick out an engagement ring. He shook his head at his foolishness. If he knew Shari, she'd want to pick out her own ring.

He was so excited, he didn't even stop at his own apartment, but sprinted up the additional flight, his suit bag bouncing against his thigh, the roses clutched in his grip. He must look like the biggest idiot on two legs, but he didn't care, he was filled with urgency to see her, to kiss her, to talk to her and to love her until morning.

Even though her phone didn't seem to be working, she must be expecting him. They hadn't spent a night apart, except last night, since they'd first made love two weeks ago. He wouldn't have believed he could find love so quickly, but the truth was, he'd loved her before he even realized it.

As he burst through the fire door onto her floor, he wondered if she'd be naked and surrounded by candlelight when he got there. He really hoped she would be. He wanted to show her he was capable of other responses when confronted by her naked, sexy body than passing out.

By the time he got to her door he was already hard, ardently anticipating their reunion after a full night's absence.

There was a note on her door, handwritten on hole-punched, lined paper. School paper, he thought with a grin. The note was in block letters, the lines wavy, as though she'd written them in a big hurry.

When he got close enough to read the words, the grin froze on his face.

Dear Lance Flagstaff

She'd underlined the name three times. He could feel the fury in the way the pen had actually scratched right through the paper in places.

He felt as if he'd swallowed all twelve prickly rose stems.

Do not attempt to contact me ever again.

19

LUKE CURSED softly and violently.

She must have seen the show. But how could she have? She'd been at school. Had someone who'd seen them together watched the show? That must be it. He was deep in it now, and he had a feeling a few roses weren't going to smooth his way.

His erection drooped, tacitly acknowledging it wasn't going to be seeing much action tonight.

Luke wiped a prickle of sweat from his forehead, fighting down panic.

She was mad. Fair enough. She deserved to be. He should have told her he'd written the damn book, and he hadn't. But he bet whatever busybody had got on the hot line to tell her that her loverboy was on television promoting his book had neglected to tell Shari that he'd announced his love for her to all of America. Didn't that count for something?

Determined to set her straight, he knocked softly on the door.

Nothing.

He knocked louder.

Nothing.

He banged his fist until it was numb and he was getting pins and needles up his arm.

Still nothing.

Dread was turning to irritation. Couldn't she at least hear him out?

He put his mouth to the door and yelled, "Shari!"

A door opened, all right, but it wasn't hers. Down the hall, Mr. Forrester, nosy old busybody, poked his head out into the hallway. "What is all this racket? At this time of night?"

Luke glanced at his watch. It wasn't even eight o'clock.

"Have you seen Shari?"

The old man's eyes narrowed, but it wasn't as if he hadn't seen them together every day. "She's probably in bed. Came home early with a cold."

So that's how she'd known.

Still, not all the cold medicines in the world would make her sleep this soundly.

He did his best to look like an anxious suitor. Hell, it wasn't difficult. That's what he was. "I only want to give her these." He flashed the roses at the busybody. "And make her some tea."

"Humph. Wish somebody wanted to make me tea," said the old man, shutting the door with a snap.

"Shari!" he yelled again, as loud as he could, banging on the door once more. "Open up or I'll—" What he'd planned to threaten if she didn't open up remained a mystery, since the door did open. To the full three inches allowed by the security chain.

Shari was on the other side of the chain, and it might as well have been a thousand miles of uncrossable ice.

"Will you stop banging on my door," she said in a furious voice, somewhat lacking in dramatic punch from the hoarse quality of her words, and the fact that she ended on a cough.

Immediately he forgot his own agenda. "You sound awful. Can I make you some tea? Or heat some soup or something?"

"There is one thing you can do for me."

"What? Anything?"

"Drop dead."

Fortunately, his reflexes were quick. He had his foot in the door before she could slam it.

"Please, listen to me."

"What for? More lies?"

"No! Shari, I love you." Okay, so it wasn't said tenderly on bended knee, while tears of joy filled his beloved's eyes. It was said while tears threatened to fill his own eyes—from the pain in his foot where she was pushing all her body weight and the door against it. If he'd had any idea he'd be in this situation, he'd have worn steel-toed boots instead of well-used sneakers.

"Will you please stop trying to break my foot?"

"Will you please go away?"

"I only want to talk to you. Just for a minute."

She was a bright woman—he'd always liked that about her, and she must be able to work out for herself that he wasn't going anywhere until she let him explain himself.

She undid the chain, let go of the door and turned back into her apartment so fast that he almost fell flat on his face when the tug-of-war ended.

The roses hadn't retained any more dignity than he had from all the pushing and shoving. He stuck them in her general direction, anyway. ''I brought you these.''

She crossed her arms across her chest and remained where she was, three feet away from the door, glaring at him.

Awkwardly, he placed the flowers in her umbrella stand, hoping she'd rescue them once he left. It seemed a shame for innocent roses to be sacrificed because she was angry.

''What do you want?''

''You!'' It wasn't suave, and it wasn't smooth. It wasn't even well thought out. But it was the raw, bare truth, and he needed her to believe it so much it hurt. ''I need you.'' He shoved a hand through his hair and tried to pull his thoughts together into some coherence, but like the curls he'd detested since he was a kid, they insisted on tossing themselves wherever they pleased.

From her unmoving stance it was clear she wasn't buying his argument.

''I owe you an apology. I should have told you I wrote that book. But, at first, all I wanted to do was to find out whether it would work. I wrote it in the first place because it was good money, but I didn't believe a book could teach a person how to be a better lover.''

''You made a fool of me.'' She said it as though the words were ripped from her throat against her will.

''No.'' He stared at her in complete disbelief. How could she believe that? ''I would never do that to you.''

'''How do you like to be touched, Shari? Do you

like this? Does that work for you?'' She mimicked
him cruelly, and only then did he see her pain. She
really believed he'd been toying with her.

"Please. Please don't believe that. Not of me, and
certainly not of yourself. I thought you'd figured it
out just the way I did. It wasn't the book that taught
us to be great together. We taught each other. We fell
in love and that's what made the sex special.''

She made a gagging noise when he got to the love
part. And that started a coughing attack, which had
her hunting in his robe pocket for a tissue. *His* robe,
which filled him with hope. She had a perfectly good
housecoat of her own, but she'd chosen to bundle
herself up in his robe when she wasn't feeling well.
That had to be good.

He glanced from the robe to her flushed face,
heavy, sad eyes and red nose. She needed looking
after, not emotional trauma.

But he couldn't let her go if she was thinking those
awful things about him. He leaned his back against
her front door and tried to explain how he'd ended
up in this mess.

"Remember the day you brought me that envelope
and the book fell out?''

"Vividly.'' He wished her hoarse voice didn't
sound so sexy. It was turning him on something awful. Which was the last distraction he needed when
he was practically fighting for his life here.

"That was the first time I'd seen the book in print.
I was horrified that you thought I'd sent for it, and
almost told you then that I'd written the damned
thing.''

"And you didn't because?" she asked with false sweetness.

"I didn't because I was embarrassed, frankly. I'd written it basically for the money. I mean, I still did the best job I could, but that's what it was. A job." He shifted his weight and dropped his suit bag at his feet so he didn't feel so weighted down. "I didn't believe a book could teach a person how to be a good lover. I pretty much figured the only way to learn was to get out there and have lots of practice. Like sports."

Her lips narrowed alarmingly, and it occurred to him that a sports analogy probably wasn't going to win him brownie points with a woman who had just accused him of playing with her emotions.

"In my arrogance—" he grinned at his own conceit and found his companion didn't share his amusement, so he stashed the grin "—I thought no one would believe I needed a book like that. So it was a bit of a shock when it was pretty obvious you did believe it.

"And that's when it hit me. The best way to prove to myself whether the book was worth the paper it was printed on was to give it a trial run."

She made a noise like a scalded cat.

"I didn't really know you," he added hastily. "You were just a sexy woman I'd been fantasizing about while I wrote the last few chapters of the book. I'd planned to ask you out, but I had a pile of deadlines that had built up while the book took up all my time. I was just getting clear of them when you came down and the book fell out." He winced in retrospect.

"You have no idea what that did for my ego, seeing you believe I needed that book."

"Just as you can have no idea what it felt like for me watching you tell all of America about your little experiment."

Damn, had he said that? He didn't entirely remember everything he'd said on Ginger's show. What with the hot lights, the noisy studio audience, his nerves at finally being outed as Lance Flagstaff...the whole thing was a bit of a blur. One thing he did remember clearly, however.

"I also told all America that I love you."

"That was nothing but phony P.R."

He understood her feelings, sympathized with them even, but this was too much. Anger speared through his groveling. "What the hell are you talking about? I love you. I told every viewer on that show and now I'm telling you, if you hadn't already figured it out. I love you and I want to marry you."

Maybe other proposals had been made at the top of the lungs in extreme frustration, he didn't know. He only knew that his first effort at asking a woman to be his wife had been made so loud they'd be hearing him in Oregon. And for all his bellowing, Shari didn't look inclined to say yes.

She shook her head. "Yesterday, those words would have meant everything in the world to me."

"What about today?"

"Have you ever heard the expression, 'A day late and a dollar short'? Go home, Luke. I'm tired and sick."

"I'm sorry," he said, not knowing what else to say.

She sighed heavily. "I'm sorry, too. I thought you were the man I'd been looking for all my life."

"I am that man," he said frantically. He'd spent most of his life working to make sure no woman ever looked at him as the man she'd been waiting for all her life. Now he knew that if Shari stopped thinking he was that man, his life would lack any meaning at all.

"I am so angry with you." She clenched both fists as she said it and he actually felt the heat of her rage.

"I told you I love you. I want to marry you. Doesn't that mean anything?"

She shot him a contemptuous glance. "It means you don't know any more about love than your father does. News flash! When you love someone you don't lie to them, you don't use them as an experiment to...to prove your stupid book works."

He threw up his hands and yelled right back at her. "All right. You don't believe me. I give up!"

He yanked the door open, picked up his suit bag and left.

He'd barely gone a step when he heard the door open again behind him. With the wild hope that she'd decided to give him another chance surging in his belly, he turned back, only to watch his roses come flying out the door behind him, end over end like a dozen red-costumed circus acrobats flipping in perfect synchronization.

As they flopped to the industrial beige carpet in the apartment hallway, he thought about just leaving them there to die, but somehow he couldn't do that, not when they'd started the evening with him in such high hopes.

He knelt to retrieve the roses and walked to nosy Mr. Forrester's door and knocked.

When it opened, he said, ''Here. Give these to your wife.''

20

SHARI HAD NEVER BEEN so angry in her life. The worst thing emotionally she'd ever dealt with before this was when B.J. stole her boyfriend and she went around baring her misery for all to see. Next to Luke's betrayal, the B.J. caper was a minor felony.

In variations of pain, losing Randy was a hangnail compared to this feeling that her heart had shattered into jagged shards, each one scraping and slicing at her tender innards.

Groaning at her own hyperbole, she decided she was in a lot of pain.

Even though her health improved, her energy level hadn't pick up. At least she'd grown up enough to not broadcast her pain to all and sundry. They probably put her heavy red eyes and lack of energy down to her recent bout with the flu. Only Therese knew the truth.

She dragged herself home Friday and, just remembering how she and Luke had spent every Friday since the day the book fell out of the envelope, had her alternately blushing with embarrassment and fuming with outrage.

She ought to go out, but she didn't want to go out. She could manage to fake it through the day, but socializing with adults would be too painful.

Therese had invited her to go along with her and her new "friend" Brad to a movie, but Shari couldn't imagine anything more depressing than being caught in the middle of that blossoming romance. It was the only bright spot in her miserable existence. Brad had embraced her suggestion that he only try to be friends with Therese. Now Therese was complaining that she couldn't seem to seduce him.

Shari thought it was great that they were getting to know each other again before jumping into bed, and if she weren't so miserable she'd be secretly smiling at how eager Therese was to get back to intimacy with that Olympic-gold-medal tongue.

But then she'd recall her own recent experience with superb sex and cringe with humiliation.

No. She was better off alone. She might as well get used to it, she thought dismally. She should probably think about getting a cat so she'd have something warm to cuddle up to now that she'd sworn off men.

She got home and checked her answering machine. No messages.

Fine. It was a good thing Luke hadn't left a message. He'd understood that her goodbye was final. Still, the fact that he'd done no groveling at all, and hadn't once left a message or tried to contact her in two days only proved she was right and he hadn't loved her at all.

She hoped his book was keeping him warm at nights. Or perhaps he already had a new woman on his hook. Teaching him to be a better lover. Ha!

She tossed her bag onto the couch with all her strength and opened the freezer. All those neat little single-girl packets of frozen home-cooked food depressed her somehow. She wasn't hungry anyway.

Maybe she'd go out and rent a movie. But what was the point? She'd choose a chick flick that ended up at happily-ever-after and she'd spend a sleepless night rewriting the ending in her head, killing off the movie star hero.

Perhaps she'd get a war movie…where a lot of men died in the end. And she'd get dinner out somewhere. Sitting alone on a Friday was not healthy.

She grabbed her bag and headed for the door. She'd already opened it and was in the hallway when she noticed Luke standing there.

Damn her rotten timing. If she'd waited, he'd have knocked and she could have squinted at him through the peephole then ignored him.

Why did it have to hurt so much to see him? And why did she want to throw herself into his arms at the same time she wanted to knee him hard in the groin?

"Hi," he said.

"I'm on my way out." She pulled herself up to her full five feet seven inches and glared down her nose at him.

"I brought you some mail."

He held out a sheaf of papers, and she took them automatically, too busy trying not to notice how painful it was to look at him to spare any attention for the mail. He looked tired and his eyes were bloodshot, as though he hadn't been sleeping well. Good. Neither had she.

When her fingers encountered papers, she glanced down, not sure what she was looking at.

Puzzlement pulled her brows together. "What is this?"

"It's *Prisons of the Mind*. I changed the ending."

They'd argued heatedly one night over Luke's insistence that Jenkins and the psychiatrist couldn't end up together. It wouldn't be realistic, he'd said, and she remembered feeling it was somehow vital to make him understand that love was the one thing that could cure Jenkins. She'd been able to see that, and she figured that psychiatrist was smart enough to see it, too. But Luke wouldn't have it.

"Why did you change it?"

Luke glanced up and down the corridor and asked if they could discuss it inside.

She wasn't nearly done being angry with him yet. "No. Here is fine. I'm going out, remember?"

He exhaled a breath noisily. "Because you were right. Love can sometimes fix a truly screwed-up guy. Take me, for instance." He rubbed the bridge of his nose. "There's been a lot of…response to my appearance on the 'Ginger' show."

Just being reminded of that horrible, humiliating program had her shoulders tensing. "Lots of women calling you up for private lessons?"

His eyes narrowed. "Sometimes you can be a real pain in the ass."

"Then why do you insist on bothering me?"

"Because," he said in the tone of one goaded past reason, "I love you."

They glared at each other for a moment. She was tempted to sweep past him on the way to her exciting evening at the video store, but was more curious about the book contract. What on earth was Luke up to?

After a moment's silence he continued. "As I was saying, there was a lot of response. The how-to book's sold out everywhere and going back for another printing."

She almost congratulated him, but then remembered how mad she was and how he didn't deserve her praise, so she kept her mouth shut.

"Meanwhile, my agent called, and I've got an offer for *Prisons*. But I knew I couldn't send it until I'd changed the ending."

He reached out and took her hand. "It's not my dad, Shari. You made me realize that. When I fell in love with you it was different from anything I've ever experienced with anyone else." He laughed shortly. "You know what I've missed most this week?"

She shook her head, but she was pretty sure it was that section of chapter eleven they'd decided to try a second time because the first time had been so much fun.

"I missed not being welcome to come make you tea and rub your feet when you were sick."

She grimaced. "You didn't miss much. I felt hideous and looked worse."

"I know." When she glared at him, he only laughed. "I mean, I didn't care that your nose was red and your eyes were watery. I only wanted to look after you. I've never felt like that before. I imagine you pregnant with our child, and I get goose bumps. I imagine you old, with gray hair and wrinkles, and I see this vibrant older woman I'll be proud to spend my life with."

She blinked her eyes rapidly and hoped he'd assume it was still the cold making her tear up.

"I went for a beer with my dad the other night and we had a long talk. One we should have had a while ago, I guess. You know what I think? I don't think he's ever really loved a woman. Maybe he doesn't have it in him. He loves all his ex-wives and kids in an easy sort of way, but I don't think he's got sticking power."

"And you do?"

"You can bet your life on it."

In fact, that was what he was asking her to do. This was her place-your-money-and-make-your-bet moment. Was he a good gamble?

She cocked her head and studied him, the usually lazy green eyes so sharp and serious. And so anxious for her answer. She suddenly realized it didn't matter all that much what her head said about it, her heart had already placed everything she had on Luke Lawson to win.

"Come on inside," she said, stepping back and opening her apartment door.

"Are you planning what I hope you're planning?"

"I'm going to let you make me some tea and rub my feet while I read your book," she told him.

She didn't get more than a step before strong male arms hauled her back. She turned to him and he kissed her, deeply and hungrily but with an aching tenderness.

"Tell me the words," he said. "I need to hear them."

Tipping her head back so she could look deep into his eyes, she said, "I love you."

"You know, you taught me to love."

Her smile was warm and open and promised him everything he'd ever wanted and hadn't known he was missing. "I'm a great teacher."